Trey's Journey

Trey's Journey

Donald L Marino

AUTHOR'S INK

Copyright © 2025 by Donald L Marino
All rights reserved. No part of this book may be reproduced in any manner whatsoever without written permission except in the case of brief quotations embodied in critical articles and reviews.
First Printing, 2025

Prologue

Trey smiled at his god mother; she returned his smile. His usually large upright frame now seemed to be hanging low.

"So, honey, what is this new journey you are on?" Ruth looked passed him out the door at Carl and James walking to their car.

"Can we sit?" Trey pointed toward a booth.

"Ok." Ruth nodded and moved toward where he had pointed.

Trey slid on the other side of the table; he noticed his hands were shaking. He half smiled hoping his aunt hadn't noticed.

"Hey, there gang. Can I get you all some of our world class Pippen hot coffee?" Mary Jean smiled at them as she laid menus down.

"Yes, black please." Trey answered quickly.

"I'll have a hot tea with honey please." Ruth responded.

"I'll be right back." Mary Jean smiled.

"So, why did you want to talk to me sweetie?"

Trey took a deep breath and thought that he might throw up.

"Oh, honey." She grabbed his hand as they laid on the table shaking. "It can't be that bad. Just relax it will be OK. Whatever it is I am here for you."

"For anything?" He smiled nervously.

"Honey, what's going on?" She released his hand.

"Here you go." Mary Jean was back with their drinks. "Are we ready to order?"

"Can you give us a few minutes?" Ruth smiled at her.

"Of course, take your time." She smiled and walked away.

"So, what is on your mind?"

"I have something to tell you." Trey stopped and lowered his head.

"Honey." She reached over and lifted his chin up so she could look into his eyes.

"I have figured something out about myself."

"Oh." She sat back and glanced over at the door then back.

"I have been lying to myself for a long time. I don't want to hurt my family. I don't want to be alone anymore either. I spent a lot of time dating the wrong ones, ones that I am not into. I love you, and I am afraid I'm going to lose you and my family."

"Honey, stop." She grabbed his hands and he stopped talking. "I understand."

"I don't know if I can say it out loud." Trey had tears in his eyes.

"Honey, you shouldn't be so hard on yourself. Be yourself and if people don't like you for that, it's their loss." She smiled at him.

"I'm gay." The words stumbled out of his mouth.

"I know. You know it's amazing how God works." She sipped her tea.

"How so?" Trey tried to pull himself together.

"If you had told me this two years ago my reaction would be totally different. I spent time on that cruise and got to know Carl and James and grew as a person."

Trey looked at her like a curious puppy.

"Yes, I still have the ability to grow. That's why God has journey's cross, it's to learn and grow."

"So, you're ok with this?"

"I am. I don't understand it, but it's not for me to understand. It's for me to love unconditionaly. I do love you, honey."

"Thank you. I love you to. Uncle Tom probably wouldn't understand would he." Trey looked sad.

"Give your God father some credit. You know he work with a fellow for years who was gay. I remember when he came home and told me that this fellow came out of the closet." She shook her head.

"What happen?"

"Well, this gentleman had been to our house a couple of times for cook outs and such. I'm not proud of this, but I said he was no longer welcome, that I didn't want someone like that around me."

"Really?"

"Like I said I have grown. He tried to tell me what I know now, but I was a little stubborn then. Looking back, I put Tom in a bad situation. He told me that this guy was one of the hardest workers he had, but I wouldn't listen. He never had a problem with him. He was so open minded and easy going. I miss him so much."

"I miss him to, but It's nice to know he would have been ok with me."

"How did your parents and brothers take this?"

Trey took another deep breath.

"You didn't tell them yet?" She smiled at him.

"This is the hardest thing I have ever done." Trey sighed.

"Do you want me to be with you?"

"Would you?"

"I will always be at your side. You're my God son and I take that very seriously."

"Thank you."

"Now let's eat. I'm told they have good food here." She picked up the menu.

Chapter One

Trey looked around the table. His dad, Ben, sat at the head of the table, and he looked just like him. In fact, his three brothers also looked just like their dad, there was no doubt who their father was. His mother, Anna, sat to the left of him. She was the opposite of the boys, she was a short blond, she had put on some pounds as she got older, but still turned heads. Next to her was his oldest brother, Stan.

Stan had gone to college to be an engineer, and that's where he met his wife Sandy, who was now sitting on the other side of him. She was feeding their baby boy, who was only six months old. She had brown hair and was just as tall as Stan, and she was in great shape, as she was a track and field star in college.

The other end of the table was the next to the oldest Eddie, he was going to a trade school to be a welder. He had no time to date as he was very focused on his work. On one side of Trey sat Clayton. He had got his cdl and was driving for a local trucking company. And on the other side of Trey sat Ruth.

"So, what is it you had to tell us?" Anna asked as she cleared plates from the table.

Trey looked around at everyone seated at the table. He had hoped it would just be his parents and Ruth there, but when the rest heard Ruth was coming, they all made time to be there.

"Is it another girl friend, God you go through them like I do underwear." Clayton elbowed him.

"I hope you change more often than, that." Ben laughed.

"That is not appropriate talk for the dinner table." Anna scolded.

Trey looked at Ruth who nodded.

"I have figured out something. Something I have known for a long time, but was too afraid to say anything." Trey said slowly.

"This sounds serious." Anna said as she sat back down at the table.

"Why would you be afraid to say something?" Ben looked confused.

Stan and his wife just looked at each other and smiled.

"I have to tell you something you may not want to hear, but I need to say it." Trey continued.

"Son, just tell us." Ben said a little frustrated.

Trey looked at Ruth, who reached under the table and held his hand.

"Mom, Dad. I'm....."

"You what?" Ben cocked his head.

"I'm gay." Trey thought he might be sick at that moment.

Everyone was silent. Trey looked around the table and noticed Stan and his wife almost smiling.

"Wait, wait, wait. What about all those girlfriends you always parade around here." Ben said as he stood.

"That was just a show, to make you happy. I was miserable."

"Maybe you just haven't found the right one yet?" Ben continued.

"Listen dad, I never did anything with any of those girls. I tried a couple of times, but I just couldn't do it." Trey started to feel a little scared.

"It's ok honey, we still love you." Anna said softly.

Ben looked at Ruth for a moment.

"You knew, didn't you?" He finally said.

"We talked at lunch today. He wants to be who he is, but he doesn't want to lose you in the process." She said as she stood and went over to his dad.

Ben turned and started to pace back and forth. "You were supposed to take over the farm. How are you going to do that?"

"I still want to do that."

"A gay guy running a farm. Can they do that?" Ben asked as he continued to pace.

"Don't be silly Ben." Ruth said as she moved in front of him. "Don't be narrow minded and destroy your relationship with Trey."

He looked over at Trey who was shaking with fear.

"I don't know what I'm supposed to do here." Ben looked at his wife, who had no words.

"Trey why don't you and I go for a walk." Stan said as he stood. Let this sink in a little for them.

Trey looked around and his mother motioned for him to go. Trey stood and followed Stan out the screen door and off the porch.

"That was very brave of you." Stan said after they were out of ear shot of the house.

"I don't feel brave, I feel sick." Trey took a deep breath.

"You could have just kept it to yourself and seen who ever on the side."

"Then I would have been living a lie. I want my family to know who the real me is."

"Like I said it was very brave of you."

Trey stopped and looked at Stan.

"What?" Stan stopped a few steps in front of him and looked back.

"Why were you and Heather almost smiling, when everyone else was in shock?"

"I have something to tell you."

"OK."

"I played around in college. I tried both teams and like both teams."

"What?" Trey couldn't believe what he was hearing.

"Heather knows this, and is ok with it."

"So, you have a boyfriend on the side?"

"No, I'm married to her now. She knows I have been with guys though."

"I don't know what to say."

"You have to be true to yourself. You never know who you will fall in love with, or when."

"I know I'm not attracted to women."

"That's a start. I am attracted to both. I fell in love with a woman, it could just as easily have been a guy, and I would have been ok with that."

"Do mom and dad know?"

"Mom does, we had a long talk about it."

"What about Clayton and Eddie?"

"Neither one of them seem interested in either sex right now, they are both tied up in their work."

"Did you talk to them?"

"No. Do I think they will be ok with you, eventually."

"What do I do now?"

"Now, you continue to be you. Dad still needs you here, the farm will be yours eventually."

"What if dad throws me out."

"Well, I don't see that happening. He may be cold for a little while as he processes things, but mom will be on your side."

"How do you know that?"

"We have talked about you. All the girlfriends, and other things we saw. I figured this day was coming and so did mom."

"I didn't hide it as well as I thought."

"Don't worry neither did I. Mom knew when I went to talk to her."

"So, if I need to talk, or advice?"

"I'm always here for you little brother." Stan stopped and looked at Trey who had a big smile on his face. He stepped forward and gave him a big hug. "Your journey may be a rough one, but those usually produce the best results."

"Thank you." Trey stepped back.

"Let's get back. Mom and Heather will have reasoned with them by now."

"Aunt Ruth too."

"The whole family at once. You are a brave soul." Stan slapped him on the back as they walked.

Chapter Two

Trey walked slowly into the kitchen where his mother was washing dishes. Her back was to him as she looked out the window.

"Ruth left for home already. She said if you need to talk, you can call her anytime." She said without looking back.

"Oh, OK." He looked at the table.

"There are pancakes and sausage in the microwave for you."

"Everyone is out early today." Trey said as he started the microwave.

"Yes, well your father didn't sleep well, and I told him I would like some time with you alone this morning."

Trey looked around.

"Clayton went back on the road this morning, and Eddie went back to school."

"I see." He pulled his food out and sat down at the table.

She laid the towel over the edge of the sink neatly, turned and leaned against it with her arms folded. She watched him as he took a bite of sausage.

"I'm sorry." He said slowly figuring he was supposed to say something but not sure what.

"I don't want you to be sorry." She unfolded her arms and sat down beside him.

"What is it you want?" He asked as he laid his fork down.

"Why is it you didn't feel comfortable coming to me?" She looked hurt.

"I didn't know what I would do if you said you didn't love me anymore."

"Do you really think I would ever stop loving you?"

"Honestly?"

She just looked at him, a look that said she always wanted honesty.

"I haven't been loving myself very much, so how could I be sure that anyone else would?"

"Why wouldn't you love yourself?"

"I'm letting you and dad down."

"The only way you would be letting us down, is by not being yourself."

"Are you sure dad feels that way?"

"Of course he does. He has a harder time showing it is all."

"So, you are ok with who I am?"

"Yes, we may not understand it, but it's not for us to judge."

"Thank you." He smiled and started eating again.

"So, who is he."

"Who?"

"The reason you came out to everyone."

"I'm not seeing anyone."

"I thought for sure there was someone. So why did you choose to come out?"

"I want to find someone. I'm lonely, and want to be with someone that makes me happy."

"I see."

"I don't want to have to hide him when I find him."

"You know your old mom is more open minded than you think, I'm glad you have a connection with your God mother, but you can always talk to me." She smiled and patted his arm.

"I'm sorry mom, I didn't mean to hurt you."

"No, no you didn't hurt me. I just want you to know that I am here for you."

Trey smiled, he knew she was lying, and that it bothered her, that he went to Ruth first. He felt bad that it never crossed his mind she would feel this way.

"Your father will be waiting for you at the barn. He said something about the hay needing to be done before it rains tonight." She smiled and got up taking his plate as he finished and got up to leave as well.

"Ok, mom. Love you." He smiled and turned to leave.

"You know I want to be part of your life, your whole life."

"I know mom."

"So, when you find someone, I want to meet him."

Trey stopped and turned back and looked at her.

"I do. I mean that."

"Thank you, mom." He smiled and headed out the door. He wasn't out the door right and his dad was there with the tractor.

"Jump on the wagon. We got to get that hay done. Rain is coming in earlier than they thought." His dad barked as he always had when the weather man was wrong and messed up his day.

They worked through lunch as the bailer broke down again. Trey fixed it enough that they could finish the fields before the rain hit. He figured he could work on it in the barn while it rained and fix it better.

It was after three when they were putting the last of the bails in the barn and the rain began.

"Beat it again." His dad said as he grabbed a coke and sat on the edge of the wagon.

"We make a great team." Trey grabbed his own coke and joined him.

There was an awkward moment as this was the first time, they had stopped moving all day.

"Are you ok son?" His dad finally asked throwing his empty bottle in a nearby plastic barrel.

"Yeah, I think I am. For the first time in a while." He stopped not sure how much to say.

"I'm sorry I didn't handle what you said very well." He scratched his head.

"I understand, it's fine. We don't have to talk." Trey said as his dad started to pace.

"Listen I know you can still do the work, that you are you no matter what." He took a deep breath.

"I am." He waited to see where this was going.

"It's just I can't picture you with a guy, doing...." He stopped.

"Good I don't want you thinking about that." Trey jumped off the wagon, ready to bolt not liking where this conversation was going.

"Well, no I didn't mean it that way." He held up his hands.

Trey stopped and looked at him. "I know it's hard. I am struggling myself. I know what I am attracted to and I know what will make me happy."

"Then that is all I can ask is that you're happy." He half smiled at him.

"I will be when I find him, I'm happy that I can be myself for now."

"I'll be honest with you. I may have a hard time at first. I mean when you bring whoever around."

"I know."

"Your mom on the other hand seems to be doing much better with this."

"Yeah."

"I just, well I guess always felt I raised a man."

"I am a man that you raise, and I live by what you taught me."

"I know I didn't mean it that way. Words always seem to get me in trouble."

"Let's cross the bridge of me being with someone when we come to it. For now, I am happy that you accept me for me."

"You're my son. I will always love you. Now enough sappy stuff. Let's get this baler fixed right."

They both worked on the baler, and just as they finished, they were being called for dinner.

Chapter Three

It had only been three days since he came out, but Trey woke looking at the empty space beside him in bed and wished he had someone there. He was feeling so lonely his heart ached.

"How do I meet a gay man?" Trey spoke into his phone, and several apps came up.

"Grinder. OK here we go." He downloaded it and set it up. He held up his phone and took a selfie.

"Not bad." He said as he looked at it. "Well, there we go it's set up."

He got around and went to the barn where his dad was waiting. Things between the two were still a little weird with his dad never knowing what to say most of the time.

He was getting a drink later that morning and his phone went off. He looked and someone had messaged him on grinder.

"HI daddy, I'm a bad boy that needs punished." Was what the message read.

Trey groaned and deleted the message. Over the next several days he received more messages that made him groan and wish he had never down loaded this site. He was sitting on the porch swing one night, deleting yet another message.

"What's wrong honey?" Anna said as she sat on the swing beside him.

"I'm lonely." He smiled and lowered his head.

"Oh, honey you'll find someone."

"It's not easy mom. Where do I go?"

"What are you looking for?"

"I want someone to grow old with, someone to take care of and share my life with."

"So, you a daddy looking for a boy?"

"What?"

"Oh, sorry, do you prefer bear looking for a cub?"

"Mom!"

"What?"

"How do you even know those terms?"

"I have google."

"Oh my God."

"I'm just trying to be supportive."

"I'm going to my room." He half smiled at her and shook his head.

She watched him leave feeling bad that her baby was lonely. She thought for a moment then snapped her fingers, smiled and walked into the house.

The next morning, he walked into the kitchen and his dad was making breakfast.

"Where is mom?" He looked around as his dad sat down with eggs and toast on his plate.

"She had an early appointment for something or other. She left smiling."

He looked around and his dad pointed toward the stove where the frying pan and eggs sat. He walked over and started to make himself breakfast. His dad finished fast.

"I'll see you at the barn." He smiled and left without waiting for an answer.

He sat down slowly and began to eat. He really wished things would go back to the way they were with his dad. They hardly talk at all anymore.

"Oh good, you're still here." Anna said smiling as she walked in.

"I was just finishing up." He said as he sat his plate in the sink.

"I told your dad that you need to be getting cleaned up by three today."

"Why?"

"Because I got you a date."

"You what!?"

"Yes, I remembered that my one girlfriend at the hair salon said her nephew was gay. I went to talk to her this morning and we called him."

"What?" Trey was mortified.

"He can't wait to meet you. His name is Brian."

"I can't believe this."

"I know you're welcome. He is a few years younger than you."

"Is he legal?"

"Yes, I believe he is eighteen or nineteen."

"You set me up with a teenager?"

"You said that you wanted a boy."

"I never said that."

"You said you wanted someone to take care of."

"I'm going to the barn."

"Be back here by three so you can get cleaned up. You want to look good."

He groaned and stopped realizing what she had said when she came in.

"Did you say you told dad about this?"

"Yes, I didn't want him to be surprised."

He hung his head and walked out the door.

"By three, I got you a new outfit." She yelled after him.

"An outfit to wear on a blind date my mother set up, a blind date I am on with my parents. Could things get any worse?"

"So, dad says you are bringing a date to dinner tonight." He looked to see Clayton walking up behind him.

"Oh, good you're home." He kicked at the dirt now.

"So, where did you meet him?" He was trying to be funny.

"I didn't."

"What?" Clayton was confused.

"Mom set this up."

"Wait mom set you up on a blind date, and the date is dinner with your family."

"Yes."

"Oh, that's so embarrassing."

"Thank you for the update."

"For you I mean, for me this is like the best Christmas gift ever."

"Glad you are enjoying this."

"Well dad asked me to help him today, saying you had things to do."

"What?"

"Trey, Clayton is going to help me today. I know you have things to do today."

"Dad, I'm fine."

"It's cool. Just enjoy your day. Come on Clayton, we got a lot to do."

Trey stood there watching them walk off as they laughed and joked. He hadn't laughed like that with his dad since he came out. He suddenly wished he had never come out.

Chapter Four

"Honey why aren't you wearing the outfit I bought you?" His mother looked at him as he came down stairs.

He had spent the day at the Laurel Mall, walking around wishing he had never come out. Hurt by his dad and confused by his mother. He wished he had someone who understood him. He was home by three to get ready for his date, not that he wanted to.

"Mom when have you ever seen me wear flowered shirts and sandals?"

"I thought you would want to play the part." She smiled at him.

"Play the part? I'm not trying out for a play, this is my life and I'm not changing who I am."

"I'm sorry honey, I'm just trying to help."

"Mom, you don't have to try so hard. Just being here for me is enough."

"OK, well he should be here soon."

"It's only four. What time did you tell him?"

"I said dinner would be at five."

"OK, we are here." His dad said as he and Clayton walked in.

"Go get cleaned up." She waved her hand at them.

"You excited?" Clayton smiled at him.

"No." Trey groaned.

They went upstairs and Trey sat down at the table.

"Honey, try and smile." She looked at him as she fried chicken.

"I'll try."

Fifteen minutes later his dad and Clayton came back down stairs all cleaned up.

"Don't you look nice." Anna smiled at them.

"Knock, knock anyone home?" Came a high voice from the front door. They all looked at each other confused.

"Hello." Clayton said as he walked to the door.

"Hi, I'm Brian." Came the high-pitched voice as Clayton got to the door.

Trey looked at his mom, horror on his face, and she shrugged her shoulders.

"Oh, Trey is in the kitchen. This way." Clayton said as he opened the door.

"Hi you all." A skinny boy walked into the kitchen. He was wearing short shorts, and flannel shirt tied into a knot at his belly. His blond hair had streaks of pink in it. He was wearing cowboy boots and a choker. Clayton was walking behind him with a big smile on his face. His dad just looked like he wanted to run.

"Well, hello." His mom said as she set the fried chicken on the table.

"Trey so nice to meet you." He held his hand out flat, like he wanted Trey to kiss his hand. Trey just stood up, took his hand and shook it.

"Oh, well you're a stocky one." He smiled.

"Well, let's sit and have dinner." His dad said as he sat and reached out his hands.

Brian just looked confused for a moment and they took each other's hands.

"We pray before we eat dear." Trey's mom said smiling.

"Oh, how retro." Brian smiled and took Trey and Clayton's hands. Trey thought he was holding a dead fish and it made him even more uncomfortable than he already was.

His dad prayed and then they all started eating. Trey's mom motioned to him.

"Would you like some chicken?" Trey offered gingerly.

"Oh, no. I don't eat meat or dairy. The animals don't want to die just so I can eat them." Brian smiled.

"Would you like some rolls?" His dad offered fighting back what he really wanted to say.

"Are they gluten free?" He asked as he pointed to them with one finger.

"I made them myself this morning." Anna said proudly.

"Oh, how old fashion, I love it, but I think I'll have to pass."

They all just looked at each other as they all had chicken and rolls at various stages of eaten.

"These mixed veggies look good." Brian took one small spoon full.

They all continued to eat as they looked at him and then at each other. Two minutes later Brian finished.

"Well, I am stuffed." Brian said. And Trey's mom looked shocked. She had been cooking all day to make a nice dinner.

"I made a chocolate cake with peanut butter icing."

"Oh, I don't eat sweets. Still got a couple pounds to lose."

Trey stopped eating his chicken and laid it down.

"Why don't we go for a walk? You can walk off some of what you ate." Brian smiled at Trey, who looked at his mom for help, she was none.

"I guess so." Trey slowly got up.

"Thanks again for dinner. I think I ate too much, I'm so full."

They walked outside as everyone else continued eating.

"So, word has it you are looking for a boy to take care of." He took Trey's hand in his.

"I'm looking for a partner to grow old with." Trey smiled at him.

Brian took Trey's hands and pulled them up to his face to kiss them.

"Oh my god, when was the last time you had a manicure. Your nails are terrible."

"A what?"

"Have someone professional do your nails."

"No, I don't do that."

"If you're going to be my daddy, you have to get them done."

Trey stopped and looked a him.

"What?" Trey looked confused.

"Listen, I want a daddy I would be proud to take out."

"I..." Trey started.

"First the nails, then we work on this." Brian patted his belly.

"I'm not looking to change who I am." Trey said as they headed back to the porch.

"Oh, honey. If you want to date you need to look presentable."

"I'm happy the way I am."

Brian stopped and stood looking him up and down.

"Baby, the gay world is going to chew you up and spit you out. I mean the homemade food is nice, but it puts to much on right there." He pointed to his waist.

"I'm only a thirty-six waist."

"Baby, you need to be a twenty-nine if you think you're going to get a boyfriend."

"Well, I'm happy with who I am."

"Oh, honey. I want a sugar daddy, but not a daddy who eats sugar."

"Well, sorry to hear that." Trey couldn't believe what he was hearing.

"I'm going to go; this isn't going to work. It was nice meeting you." He laughed a little.

Trey just nodded, and walked him to his car.

"If you fix yourself, get in touch."

"I don't think so." Trey said as he closed his door for him. Trey turned and walked into the house not even waiting for him to leave.

"You're not into that are you?" His dad barked as he walked in.

"God no!" Trey shook his head. "I dated girls who were more masculine."

"I don't know, I think you made a cute couple." Clayton smiled.

"You want some cake?" His mother smiled holding out a plate with cake on it. She was desperately trying to change the subject.

"He looked like a daisy duke reject." Ben almost laughed.

"Please mom, don't help again." He said as he took his cake and got a glass of milk.

"What did he say to you?" Anna asked.

"Said I'm fat, and needed to lose weight and needed to get my nails done if I wanted to be his daddy." He scarfed the cake down and put the plate in the sink.

"Where are you going?"

Trey stopped and looked around. "Clayton's here, dad would rather work with him. I'm going to pack a few things and go to the trailer; I need some time alone." He headed upstairs.

Chapter Five

"Honey, can we talk for a minute before you leave?" Anna said as he came down the stairs.

Trey stopped and sighed heavy, turned and looked at her.

"I'm sorry, I didn't know he was like that."

"I know mom."

"I just wanted to help."

"I know mom."

"Your dad loves you."

"I know he is having trouble understanding. I just wish he would treat me like he always did. I'm still the same person."

"He will come around."

"I miss our time together."

"I know."

"I'm going to go now."

"Are you going to be, OK?"

"I just need some time alone."

"OK."

"You know what I wish, why I want someone?" Trey stopped as he was starting to leave.

"No."

"Because I need someone who understands me, where I'm coming from and what I am feeling. I feel so lonely."

"I'm sorry baby."

"It's not your fault. I'll figure it out." Trey left and soon he was starting a camp fire and sitting back.

Trey picked up his phone and sent a text, soon he got a text back and smiled. He cracked open a beer. Soon a car pulled up and he looked back and smiled.

"So, what is going on?" Benton said as he got out of his car.

"I just need to spend some time with someone who knows how I feel."

"So how did coming out go?"

"Well, my dad says he is ok, but it's not the same."

"And." Benton said as he opened a beer and sat down.

"My mom tried to help." Trey rolled his eyes.

"What do you mean?"

He explained what happen.

"Wow." Benton sat shaking his head.

"I feel so alone." Trey sighed.

"You're not. I'm always here. I'm sure Carl and the guys would be there for you as well."

"I don't want to be a bother." He sighed.

"Listen we all went through tuff times coming out. You need someone you can talk to."

"That's why I texted you."

"So maybe we should go out sometime." Benton offered.

"Like a date?" Trey smiled.

"No, I mean I would be your wing man."

"Wing man. That might be fun."

"I'm just not ready to date. I know Allen would want me to, but I still miss him so much."

"I know, you two were good together."

"Let's play some music and relax."

They turned on the radio drank beer and joked with each other.

"Are you staying the weekend?" Trey said as the fire died.

"I brought my bag."

"I'll go for coffee in the morning."

"Are the beds in the back room fixed?"

"Sorry, Dad took them all out. He said he is getting some used ones to put in there, but nothing yet."

Benton got his bag out of the car and they walked into the trailer. Benton sat down on the couch and fluffed the small pillow on the end of the couch.

"You can bunk with me you know." Trey smiled at him.

"I don't know that that would be a good idea."

"I didn't say anything would happen. I know you're not ready."

"Thank you, but I'll sleep here."

"OK, I'll see you in the morning." Trey smiled at him and went back the hall.

Benton laid on the couch and it was so uncomfortable, he wondered how he ever slept here. Then he remembered he was totally drunk then. An hour went by and he gave up.

"Can I still bunk in here?" Benton stuck his head in Trey's room.

"Come on." Trey slid back making room for him.

Benton laid there very relaxed and was soon asleep. Trey laid awake wanting to snuggle with him, but forced himself not to. He soon rolled over so his back was to Benton hoping he would get some sleep.

"Hey your up." Trey said as he walked in with coffee in the morning.

"Yeah, I slept well. It was nice feeling someone next to me." Benton smiled at him.

"It was nice." He handed him a coffee.

"What's in the bag?"

"I got a couple of breakfast sandwiches."

"Nice." Benton reached in and grabbed one.

"I picked up a few things for lunch and dinner. We can just hang out all day."

"I'm up for that."

Trey was glad to hear that. He knew what Benton had said, but he secretly hoped he could get him to change his mind. Benton was exactly what he was looking for. He smiled as Benton ate and drank his coffee. It made him feel so good to take care of him.

"What are you smiling about?" Benton caught him.

"Nothing, just having a nice time for a change. It feels good."

"It is good to be with close friends." Benton went outside.

"What are you doing?"

"We need to get wood for the camp fire later." Benton smiled at him.

Trey smiled thinking about the first time Benton had been here. He had no idea what to do for a camp fire and now he was all about doing it himself. They worked together and got enough wood together for the night.

Trey made them lunch after which they sat on the lawn chairs relaxing.

"Let's play basketball." Trey got up and grabbed the ball off of the porch.

"You know I'm not athletically inclined." Benton smiled at him.

"Come on, I suck at basketball too, anyway it will give us something to do."

Benton sighed and got up. They played slowly at first then they started to play more aggressively and talking trash. Both were terrible and hardly ever made a basket. They were sweating after a while; Trey went for a basket and Benton didn't move. Trey knocked him down and tripped falling right on top of him. They were both laughing and Trey looked right into Benton's eyes. They held each others looks for several moments, then Benton laughed slightly.

"Are we going to stay here all day?" Benton finally said as it seemed Trey wanted to kiss.

"Oh yeah sorry." Trey got to his knees and playfully slapped Benton's face. "I think I won."

"You didn't even make a basket." Benton laughed.

"Neither did you, and I was the closest." Trey laughed and grabbed a beer out of the cooler.

"I'm thirsty to." Benton said getting up.

"Catch." Trey tossed a beer to him.

They drank a few beers and then lit the camp fire.

"I love camp fires." Benton smiled.

They made small talk for a while. Roasted hot dogs on sticks, listen to music and danced around.

"Ah, listen a slow song." Benton said as he went to sit down.

"May I have this dance?" Trey smiled at him and held out his hand.

"Really?" Benton smiled at him.

"Yeah, why not?"

Benton took his hand and Trey pulled him in and led. He loved the feel of Benton against his chest as they danced. When the song was done, they both smiled, grabbed a beer, sat down not saying much. The fire slowly went out, and they finished their beer.

"I guess we should go to bed." Trey stood and stretched.

"Yeah, I'm tired." Benton said as he helped put out the last of the coals.

They walked into the trailer and Benton followed Trey back to the bedroom. They made small talk as they climbed into bed, both feeling pretty good from the beers.

"You know I was thinking." Benton said.

"Thinking what?" Trey said as he pulled the covers over his shoulders.

"If you want to snuggle." Benton smiled at him.

"Really?"

"Yes." Benton said and rolled over waiting for Trey. Trey smiled and crawled up behind him as close as he could and put his arm around him. Benton grabbed his hand and interlocked their fingers, and pulled his arm tight around him.

"Thank you." Trey whispered as he snuggled in. Soon they were both smiling as they slept.

Trey woke in the morning to find Benton wasn't in bed. Trey walked into the living room to see Benton sitting there crying.

"What's wrong?" Trey said as he sat down beside him.

"I feel like I'm cheating on Allen. I really enjoyed last night and I feel like I shouldn't have."

"I'm sorry." Trey got up and didn't know what to do. He really wanted to be with Benton, but not like this.

"I think I should go. I don't want to hurt you." Benton got up and grabbed his bag.

"Can I call you?"

"Um, well I don't know."

"How about you call me when you are ready to talk."

"OK."

Benton set his bag down and locked eyes with Trey, they stood for a moment, then Trey grabbed Benton's face with both hands and kissed him gently, and held it for several moments. When he pulled back Benton's eyes were full of tears.

"I've got to go." Benton grabbed his bag and walked out the door.

Trey stood at the door way watching Benton leave with tears in his own eyes.

Chapter Six

Trey sat on the front porch steps with his phone laying at his side. He had messaged Benton when he had got home from the trailer and apologized for kissing him. Benton said not to worry about it, he asked if they could talk. That was four days ago and still no response.

"Honey what is bothering you?" His mother asked as she sat down beside him.

"Nothing." He sighed.

She just gave him that look that told him she knew he was lying.

"What do you do when you like someone, but they don't like you back."

"Well, you can't force someone to like you. Do you like or love this person."

He just hung his head.

"So, you met a young man and he doesn't have the same feelings for you as you have for him?"

"Something like that."

"Are you sure he is gay?"

"Yes, he was married and his husband died of cancer, he feels like he would be cheating on him." Trey had tears in his eyes as he looked at his mom.

"Oh, I see. You have it bad for this young man." She put her arm around him.

"I just don't know what to do."

"There isn't much you can do. You may have to face the fact that he may never want to be with anyone else."

"I know."

"Just try being friends with him."

"It's hard to do that when he won't talk to you."

"Then you may just have to move on."

"I know, it's just so hard meeting any…" He stopped himself.

"Don't worry I'm not going to try and fix you up again."

"Before you met dad, did you ever think you may be alone for the rest of your life."

She looked at him and smiled. "Let me tell you about Terry Marshall."

"Who?"

"He was the boy I wanted to marry. He played short stop on the baseball team. He was good, scouts from a lot of big colleges were after him."

"I see."

"I was convinced that he was going to marry me. We had gone on a couple of dates. He even made it to second base."

"Mom." He smiled at her.

"In those days that made me quite a lose girl. Anyway, he said he had a big announcement and he was going to make it at the prom. I was sure he was going to give me his class ring as a promise ring. I didn't know however that the university of Miami had signed him the day before prom. He got on the stage with the band I walked up front all confident I knew what was going to happen. He made the announcement and my heart broke. Everyone was happy for him hugging him shaking his hand. I stood there watching my dream man walk away from me."

"Did he say anything to you?"

"That Monday at school, he told me that baseball was his future. He hugged me and that was how he broke up with me."

"What happen to him?"

"I never saw him again after we graduated. I think he is still playing in the minor leagues somewhere."

"So, what's the point?"

"The point is God has a plan. That night at the prom your father had congratulated him, then saw me standing there looking like I was going to cry. He came over and asked if I was ok. We left before the prom was over and went to Scoopers and had a root beer float."

"You fell in love with him then." Trey smiled.

"God no, I thought he was a big goof ball, but he used that and made me laugh. He hung around and made me laugh until I fell in love with him. He is the one I was meant to be with. You will find who you are meant to be with as well. This one may be on his way to the minor leagues and you just have to let him go."

"Thanks mom." He hugged her and headed back into the house and to bed.

"Hey little brother." Clayton said as Trey came down for breakfast.

"Good morning." Trey smiled shocked to see him home.

"I know I'm a day earlier than normal."

"Fine with me, gives me an extra day off." Trey shrugged.

"Yes, and I have something for you to do."

"What?" Trey looked scared.

"A friend of mine needs a ride along on a four-day trip to Georgia."

"So why are you asking me?"

"I thought maybe a change of scenery would be good."

Trey looked at his mom, who shrugged her shoulders, then back at Clayton, then noticed his dad was gone.

"Where is dad?"

"At the barn already." Clayton smiled.

"Oh my God." Trey sighed and shook his head.

"What?" Clayton said trying to sound innocent.

"Your friend is gay isn't he. You two are setting me up again and dad wants nothing to do with it. That's why he is out already."

"Ok, but he is really nice. You would like him. I mean he is no Brian." Clayton half laughed.

"Mom, you said you wouldn't set me up again."

"I didn't, he did." She pointed to Clayton.

"She asked me to."

"I asked if you knew anyone. You did the rest yourself."

"Four days with a guy I don't know, in a small truck."

"The trucks are pretty big."

"How well do you know him?"

"I talked to him on the radio, I met him a couple of times. He looks like a normal guy."

"What do you have to lose?" His mother smiled. "Better than moping around here."

"I can't believe you guys."

"So, after you eat, go pack. I have to have you there by noon."

Trey just stood there looking at them in disbelief.

"Here is your breakfast." His mother set eggs, bacon and pancakes on the table.

Trey sat down slowly and started to eat.

"It will be fun." His mother smiled at him. He continued to eat slowly as they both joined him eating and smiling at him.

Chapter Seven

"Why do you hate me?" Trey groaned again as they pulled into the lot where they were going to meet his friend.

"For the hundredth time I don't hate you. You are looking for someone and I'm just trying to help."

"This family is too helpful sometimes." Trey grabbed his back pack and got out of the car.

"You wouldn't have it any other way." Clayton laughed.

"Oh, Clayton there you are." A big grizzly looking man walked up to them. He had a full beard that was graying, he was over six foot tall with massive arms and a big smile.

"Hey chuck. This is my brother Trey." Clayton pointed to Trey who just stood there like a deer in head lights, dwarfed by Chuck.

"You ready boy?" Chuck said in his deep voice.

"Just a minute." Trey smiled.

"I'll go check the truck quick, don't take to long." Chuck turned and walked over to a truck close by.

"Have you lost your mind?" Trey glared at his brother.

"Mom said you were looking for a daddy."

"She has got to stay off google. I never said that."

"You'll have a good time." Clayton slapped him on the back.

"Let's go boy." Chuck yelled as he got into the truck.

"What is happening to my life?" Trey muttered as he slowly walked over to the truck and got in.

"You move slow for working on a farm boy." Chuck growled as he got in.

"Sorry, I'm just a little nervous."

"Nothing to be nervous about." Chuck smiled as he put the truck in gear and they headed out.

They road in silence for a while.

"So, Clayton says you just came out boy?"

"Yes." Trey answered. He wasn't sure how much he liked being called boy, it just didn't feel right to him.

"Your, looking for a daddy, boy?"

"Well, that may not be totally true." Trey fake smiled, there was the boy thing again.

"Well, then we will find out on this trip if that's what you want boy." He looked over and smiled at him. His smile was at least warm and made him feel a little more at ease.

"OK." was all Trey could think to say.

Chuck didn't talk much other than to curse out drivers every now and then. By six o'clock Trey really needed to use the bathroom and was getting hungry.

"Are we going to stop to eat?" Trey finally asked.

"Are you getting hungry boy?"

"Yeah, and I need to use the bathroom."

Chuck laughed. "We will stop for the night soon enough. Piss in this in the meantime." He handed him a plastic bottle.

Trey took it relieved to be able to go, but unsure if he was going to be able to with him watching. But he had to go so bad it didn't take him long. Two hours later they pulled into a truck stop. Trey threw the bottle away and went to the rest room. They got some Burger King and ate.

"You're a good-looking young man." Chuck smiled at him.

"Thank you." Trey said as he finished swallowing some of his burger.

They were walking back to the truck and Chuck grabbed Trey's ass. His big hand covering a good part of it. Trey jumped.

"That is mine boy." Chuck smiled as he held on tightly.

"OK." Trey didn't know what to say or do.

They got into the sleeper.

"Come on in close boy." He wrapped his arms around him and pulled him in close.

"You're my boy, you call me sir." He whispered in his ear.

"What?" Trey wasn't sure he heard him right.

"Always finish your sentences to me with sir."

"Really?" Trey was surprised.

"Really what?"

"Really sir?" Trey said slowly.

"That's a good boy. Be a good boy and sir won't have to punish you." He said then started to kiss his neck.

Trey thought for a minute. Did he say punish? He decided he didn't want to know. Just then he shoved his fingers in Trey's mouth.

"Has boy ever sucked on a dick before?"

"No........sir."

"Practice on my fingers. Suck on them nice and slowly." Trey did as he was told. "You're a natural."

Trey smiled a little. "Thank you, sir."

He grabbed Trey by the head and pushed him down. "Now service your daddy."

Before he knew it, he was giving him a blow job, and somehow he managed to flip Trey around and play with his ass, while Trey was blowing him.

"You're a good boy." He slapped his ass. He flipped him around again and had lube on his ass before he knew what was happening.

"I don't know." Trey started to say and he put his hand over his mouth and slowly pushed his way in. When he was all the way in, he laid on top of Trey and chewed on his neck.

"Good fucking boy. Now I'm going to fuck the crap out of you." He whispered in his ear.

The next morning Trey woke and they were already on the road.

"I needed to clean up." Trey looked out the curtain, and Chuck just gave him a dirty look.

"Sir, I needed to clean up sir."

"That's better boy, but we needed to get going, there are baby wipes back there use them. Don't sleep so long next time."

Trey sat back and was hurting from the night before. He had been really rough and Trey wasn't sure he liked it. He used the wipes and laid back down.

"Sir, I'm going to lay back here, I'm a little sore this morning and don't think I can sit right now."

Chuck laughed. "You'll get used to it boy."

A couple of hours later Trey came out and sat.

"Got to get used to the trucking life boy. We will spend a lot of time on the road, and very little at home." Chuck smiled at him.

If only the rest of him were as warm as his smiled Trey thought to himself, and he thinks we are a couple now. Trey wasn't sure what to do. It was late when they pulled into a Love's truck stop.

"Where are we?"

"By the Florida, Georga line. We will drop this load first thing in the morning. Let's go get something to eat."

Trey was thrilled by the idea. They had just eaten snacks all day.

"Maybe I should shower to." Trey smiled.

"I'm only going to make you a mess again shortly. I'll wake you in the morning." Chuck slapped him on the back.

Trey wasn't sure he could do it again, but he just smiled. They ate and again on the way back to the truck Chuck grabbed his ass, but this time he let go and slapped it so hard it knocked him forward a few steps.

"Ok, boy it's time to take care of your daddy." Chuck said as they climbed in the back. Trey sighed and smiled. Chuck grabbed him and kissed him really hard. "You're going to be such a good boy." He sat up and push him down and grabbed the back of his head and abused his throat.

"You're such a good fucking boy." He pulled him off and slid in behind him and went right at it.

"Shit!" Trey yelled, and Chuck put his fingers in his mouth and shoved them in as far as he could.

"Boy, daddy likes it raw. Don't worry you'll get used to it. You're mine now." He had his one huge arm wrapped around his neck pulling him in and making it hard to breathe, and the other hand was still in his mouth, while he pounded his ass. He finished and pushed him back down and made him suck his dick clean.

"Boy wake up." Chuck shook Trey's shoulder.

"What?" Trey rubbed his eyes. He was very tired because he just wasn't sleeping, next to Chuck.

"Wake up its morning."

"OK." Trey rubbed his eyes.

"OK what?" Chuck pulled his hair hard.

"OK, sir." Trey was shocked at how rough he was.

"Ok, boy now go down on me. I need to relieve myself this morning."

"What sir?" Trey looked back over his shoulder not sure what he was hearing.

"As my boy, you will drink my morning piss." Chuck grabbed him and started to push him down, but Trey jumped back.

"I don't think." Trey shook his head and grabbed his bag.

"Boy, don't make me punish you."

"Ok, first I don't like being call boy." Trey was now grabbing his clothes at the bottom of the bunk.

"Where are you going boy. I'm your ride and you'll do as I say."

"I don't need a ride that bad." Trey put his shirt on and was trying to get his pants on when Chuck grabbed them.

"Boy you leave this truck you don't get back in. Now just do as your told."

"I have no intention of getting back into this truck." Trey finished putting his pants on and slipped his sneakers on.

"I mean it you leave no coming back."

"I don't care." Trey went to go and Chuck grabbed his hair again.

"Boy the punishment will be really bad for you if you don't stop right now."

"Let me go, and stop calling me boy. I can't believe my brother thought I would like you." Trey pushed away and jumped out of the truck.

Trey walked into the truck stop over to the diner side.

"Hey honey, can I help you with something?" A waitress asked as she saw him sit. He looked at her and she was wearing a name tag that said Amy.

"A coffee please." Trey sighed not sure what he was going to do now. He didn't want to call home and have to explain what happen. That would be to embarrassing.

"Here is your coffee. You, ok? You look upset." She said as she sat the coffee down.

"No, yes, I'm not sure." Trey said as he fought the tears that ended up winning.

"Want to talk?" She asked as she sat across from him.

Trey looked out the window to see Chuck's truck driving away.

"Well, my brother set me up with a driver friend of his and he turned out to be a jerk, who is really weird."

"Set ups, I hate them. You need a ride home. I'll call a cab for you."

"That would be and expensive ride."

"Why, where are you from."

"North east pa."

"Oh." She patted his hand then looked up to see two guys walk in. A burly man with reddish brown hair and beard, and a younger man with strawberry blond hair.

"Well, look who the dogs have drug in." She smiled as she got up. "Ben and Trent haven't seen the two of you in a while.

"Nice to see you too." Ben smiled at her.

"It's so good to see you two still together."

"When you find someone who loves you, why look anywhere else." Trent smiled as he hugged her.

Amy looked back at Trey then smiled. "Hey are you heading north by chance."

"Yeah New York City. Just stopped for coffee."

"And to see me." Amy smiled at them, and they all laughed.

"Of course. Why do you ask?"

"That young man over there needs to get back north. The guy he was with left him or he ran from him, not sure which. Eather way I think he is happy not to be with him."

"OK." Ben put his hand up and walked over to Trey.

"HI."

"Hi." Trey looked up confused.

"I understand you need to get back up north."

"Maybe why?"

"Amy over there says you need help. Me and my boyfriend would be glad to give you a ride."

"I've been through enough weird things thank you."

"Not sure what has happened to you, but we don't play around. I'm just offering you a ride because Amy said you needed help."

"I do need help. I will pay you." Trey looked hopeful.

"You don't need to pay us. We would be glad to help."

"I could really use the help."

"Get your coffee to go, we are hitting the road."

Trey got up and Ben patted him on the back. "It's going to be OK."

Chapter Eight

Trey had crawled into the sleeper; he was tired and figured if he slept it would make the trip go by faster. He just wanted it all to be over.

His thoughts drifted, he went back to high school and the locker room the day the three of them took advantage of Benton. It made him sick now. He thought how they must have made Benton feel. He thought of Chuck and wondered how he could live with himself acting the way he did.

"Hey buddy." Came a voice through the cloudiness of his sleep.

"Hu, what?" Trey half opened his eyes.

"Are you OK?" it was the guy with the strawberry blond hair, Trey couldn't think of his name. He was still tired.

"Yeah, I think so."

"You have been saying I'm sorry over and over again."

"Really?" Trey rubbed his eyes.

"You're soaked with sweat."

Trey looked down his shirt looked like he had taken a shower.

"I'm so sorry guys." He just looked around not knowing what to do.

"It's fine." Ben said from the driver's seat.

"He must have really been a jerk to you." Trent said handing him some wet wipes.

"Something like that." Trey washed his face off.

"You want to sit up front, put the window down and get some air." Trent offered.

"That might be a good idea." Trey climbed into the front seat and put the window down some.

"Do you want to talk about it?" Ben asked glancing over at him.

"I have a lot going through my mind right now." Trey half smiled at him.

"Well, we got nothing but time, so if you need to talk, we are here."

Hours went by, Ben had put on some country music and Trey was feeling a little better.

"How is it with you guys?" Trey asked as he looked out the window.

"What do you mean?" Ben asked.

"I don't understand what all the terms mean, and why are there terms?"

"Terms?"

"Like daddy, son, bear, cub whatever why can't I just be me?" Trey finally looked over at Ben.

"Trent jokes and calls me daddy, but we are just us. We don't try to fit into a mold."

"I don't want to fit into a mold. Being gay is not all there is to me."

"Sadly, there is a portion of the gay community that don't feel that way. They need the molds to feel like they are wanted."

Trey got quite for a while and then sighed.

"What?" Ben smiled.

"Do you believe in karma?"

"I believe what you put out is what you get back. You can call it karma or whatever you like."

"I feel like karma just came to visit me."

"Why would you think that?"

"I did something I'm not proud of when I was in high school." Trey hung his head and sighed again.

"We all do stupid things. Doesn't mean bad things will happen." Ben looked to see if there was more coming, but Trey was quiet.

"Is anyone hungry, I can make some sandwiches?" Trent finally said.

"I could eat." Trey smiled.

"Ham and cheese, OK?"

"Yeah, you have mustard?"

"Yep."

"I'll take the same." Ben chimed in.

Trent made the food and got out some chips and sodas. Ben turned up the music.

They listen to music and made small talk for the rest of the afternoon.

"I think we should get a hotel room tonight." Ben said as the sun was setting.

"I'll pay for it." Trey offered.

"No, you won't. You're our guest and we will take care of you."

"Thank you." Trey sighed feeling like he was taking advantage.

An hour later they were pulling into a truck stop that had a day's inn beside it.

"We'll eat here first, and then just walk over to the hotel."

They went in and ordered and Trey excused himself to go to the bathroom.

"Excuse me miss." He stopped by the register.

"Yes, can I help you?"

"I want to pay for the bill, before my friend tries to pay for it."

"Of course."

He pulled out his credit card and paid the bill, and walked back to the table satisfied he wasn't totally a burden on his new friends.

They ate and Ben tried to pay and was told it was already paid for. He looked at Trey who just smiled. They got things from the truck and walked over to the hotel. Ben paid for the room and they all got showers. Trey felt so much better.

"You didn't have to pay for dinner." Ben said again as he joined Trey on the balcony.

"You didn't have to be so nice to me." Trey smiled at him and they looked at the clear night sky again.

"What are you thinking about?"

"Nothing really."

"When I came out, I spent a lot of time looking at the stars asking questions that I had no answers for. Hoping by some miracle of God I would get an answer."

"The answers don't come do they?" He looked back at Ben.

"They do. I got the answers I was looking for when God was ready to give them to me."

"I'm not sure God is going to listen."

"Because of the school thing?"

"Maybe."

"What happened?"

"Me and two other football players caught a boy looking at us in the shower." Trey looked off into the sky wishing it would just swallow him up.

"And." Ben asked even though he had a good idea of where this was going.

"We took advantage of him. We each took turns using him."

"I see, and you think Chuck was the karma of that?"

"I do."

"What happen to this boy?"

"We are friends now, hang out from time to time. I would love to date him."

"But, he hasn't forgiven you?"

"Well, I hadn't thought about that. He was married and his husband died of cancer, he just can't get past it."

"But Chuck made you think about what happen?"

"If I made him feel the way I felt." Trey hung his head.

"Life is full of lessons we are supposed to learn from. Sometimes we learn the hard way. It's the great thing about free will." Ben smiled at him.

"I guess."

"Listen to him, talk to this guy. Tell him your sorry. Tell him why if you want. You learned something, but you also have to move on from it.

Dwelling on it isn't going to change anything." Ben was standing beside him looking into the night sky.

"You two seem to be very happy." Trey looked back at Trent who was asleep.

"We are. I am very lucky." Ben looked at Trey

"What?"

"What about you. What are you looking for?"

"I want someone I can take care of, someone to grow old with. I want someone who is a guy, but who is gentle in the bedroom. I feel like I want the impossible."

"It's not impossible, but don't try so hard. Just keep in mind what you're looking for and the universe will hear you."

"I'm not the one trying so hard. My mom and brother are." Trey laughed a little.

"Well, we have a long day tomorrow. We will be in New York by the end of the day."

"I'll call my oldest brother in the morning I am sure he will pick me up."

"Good."

"Ben."

"Yes."

"Can we keep in touch. I don't have many gay friends that understand what I'm going through. It would be nice to talk to you two from time to time."

"I would like that. Give me your number." Ben pulled out his phone.

Chapter Nine

"Are you sure you're going to be, OK?" Ben asked as Trey got out of the truck.

"Yes, thank you for all your help. Stan is waiting for me."

Trey walked through grand central looking for Stan who texted saying he was there already.

"Trey over here." Trey looked to see Stan waving, and hurried over to him.

"Are you, OK?" He grabbed him by the shoulders and gave him a once over.

"I'm fine."

Stan gave him a big hug.

"What were you thinking going with a strange man on a truck like that?"

"Clayton said he knew him and that he was a nice guy."

"Clayton is not the best judge of character."

"I know that now." Trey smiled and they walked out of the station.

Stan lived just outside of New York City near Milford Pennsylvania. He worked in the city, but did not want to live there. They were back at his house in no time.

"Sandy is at school yet and the baby is at her mom's today. She is picking him up before she comes home. So, we have some brother time."

"I wish I had just never come out. Mom has been trying too hard to make sure I am happy, and dad doesn't know what to say to me anymore." Trey sat down at the table as Stan grabbed them each a soda.

"That's why I never said anything. That and I wasn't a hundred percent sure who I would end up with." Stan sat down.

"I don't know what to do now. Things are not the same at home, and I can't fix it."

"It's a tough road you picked." Stan sipped his soda.

"You know I thought the family would abandon me. Hate me and turn their backs on me." Trey just stared at the wall not looking at anything in particular.

"Well at least that didn't happen. That's a good thing." Stan put his hand on his arm.

"Is it? Look at what I'm dealing with now. I feel like it's just chaos all around me. I'm being set up with weird guys for what reason."

"Mom is just trying to let you know she is OK with who you are, as for Clayton he is just an ass."

"And dad?"

"He doesn't do change well. This will take him some time."

"But I haven't changed, I'm still the same person I was a month ago."

"I know that, give them time to realize that."

"I know, but I think I need a break."

"I already talked to mom. I told her you were going to stay here for a couple of days."

"Thank you." Trey smiled at him.

"I'm home." Susan announced as she came in the door.

"In the dining room." Stan replied.

"Hey honey how are you?" She walked up and kissed Stan.

"Fine thanks."

"Oh, Trey so good to see you. Stan has told me a little about what's going on."

"Yeah, it's a little crazy."

"Well, you're welcome to stay here as long as you need to." She walked over and kissed him on top of the head. She looked at Stan who smiled at her. "I'm going to get the baby down for his nap."

"Ok, honey." He looked at Trey. "I hope you don't mind we are having some friends over tonight. We had this planned two weeks ago."

"No, it's fine." Trey smiled.

"You can join or stay upstairs whatever you feel better doing. We will understand. I know it's been a rough couple of days."

"I'll join, it will be a nice distraction."

"Good, I'm glad."

"I need to get cleaned up." Trey smiled and grabbed his bag.

"You know where the bathroom is, Towels are in the closet."

"Thank you."

"Bring your dirty clothes down, we will wash them." Stan said as Trey headed up the stairs.

"OK."

Trey took his shower and was soon back down stairs.

"Just put those close in the laundry room." Sandy said to him as he hit the bottom of the stairs.

He put his clothes in the laundry room and joined them in the kitchen.

"So, what's the party for tonight."

"They work with me and once a month we go to one person's house for dinner. We each bring a covered dish." Stan said as he was prepping chicken.

"What are you making?" Trey looked confused. "That's a lot of chicken for a covered dish."

"Well, the person's house the dinner is at makes the main dish." Sandy smiled.

"So, we are doing barbeque chicken."

"Nice."

Stan was out at the grill as people started showing up. Most of them were several years older than his brother. He was introduced, but he knew he was never going to remember their names.

"Oh Trey, this is Rodney and Sara Atkenson. He is Stans boss."

"Nice to meet you." Trey shook their hands. "I'm Trey, Stan's little brother."

"Nice to meet you. This is our son Oscar." Rodney stepped aside and Oscar smiled and put his hand out. Trey blinked and took his hand and shook it. Oscar was maybe an inch shorter than Trey with black hair and brown eyes. He had olive skin just like his mothers, and his smile melted Trey a little.

"Nice to meet you." Trey said slowly.

"Nice to meet you." Oscar smiled at him as he shook his hand, and there was an electric vibe that made Trey uncomfortable.

"I think I need to get a drink." Trey smiled and headed to the patio where there were coolers with soda.

"I'll join you." Oscar said and followed, much to Trey's dismay.

Trey grabbed a soda and stood by the fence. There were a couple of guys playing horse shoes close by.

"These things can be very boring." Oscar said as he joined him.

"I see." Trey smiled a little.

"The only reason I come is for the food. They make some of the best stuff. If John's wife made her mac and cheese, it's a must." Oscar took a drink of his soda.

"So, what grade are you in?" Trey asked not knowing what else to say.

"Grade?"

"Yeah, I figured you were still in high school."

"No." Oscar laughed.

"Oh, sorry." Trey was a little embarrassed.

"I'm in my second year of college. I'll be twenty in a month."

Trey raised his eyebrows; he was only a year younger than him.

"I said I only come for the food." Oscar smiled at him.

"So, what are you going to school for?" Trey decided he wanted to learn more about Oscar.

"Business management. I want to start my own business someday."

"Very cool, what kind of business?"

"I haven't made up my mind on that yet, but I got time. What about you?"

"I work on the family farm; I will be taking it over one day."

"A farm boy." Oscar looked him up and down. "Very nice."

The two of them hung out the rest of the night. Oscar pointed out the good food. Trey was having the nicest time he had had in a long time.

"Listen would you like to keep in touch?" Oscar asked as him and his parents were getting ready to leave.

"Yeah, sure. I'll give you, my number."

Oscar pulled out his phone and put in Trey's number.

"I'll text you later. It was nice meeting you." He reached his hand out and Trey took it and shook his hand heavy. The warmth of Oscar's hand sent vides through him again.

They left and soon everyone was gone, Stan and Susan were cleaning up when Trey walked back into the kitchen.

"You look like you enjoyed yourself." Stan smiled at him.

"I did thank you very much. I'll go get stuff from the back yard." Trey helped them clean up and kept checking his phone, but no message came.

"Is something wrong?" Susan asked after she seen him looked at his phone again.

"No, nothing. I'm tired do you guys' mind if I head off to bed?"

"No, go ahead." Susan smiled.

"Goodnight." Trey smiled and headed up stairs.

"What's with him?" Stan looked confused.

"I think he thinks he made a connection." Susan smiled.

"With who?"

"Oscar. Did you see the two of them together all night?"

"No, I was too busy winning at horseshoes."

"The great victory." She laughed.

Trey laid in bed looking at his phone that never went off and soon he fell asleep. Morning came and the sun was up before Trey. He rubbed his eyes and went to the bathroom.

"Are you up?" Susan yelled up the stairs.

"Yes."

"I'm making coffee."

"Great."

Trey shuffled back to his bed and picked up his phone there was one new message. His hand started shaking and he wasn't sure he could even open his phone, but he did and it was a message from Oscar.

Sorry it took me so long to message you. I wasn't sure
if I should. Please don't get offended, but I felt something
between us and I find you cute and would like to get to
know you better.

"YES!" Trey screamed.

"Are you ok?" Susan yelled up the stairs.

"No, he will be thrilled." Stan hung up his phone as he walked up to his wife.

"Who was that?" Susan looked confused.

"My boss. Their son likes Trey."

"Trey just got a message then I take it."

"I would think so."

"Good morning." Trey said smiling coming down the stairs.

"Anything you want to tell us?" Susan smiled.

He looked back and forth at the two of them. "Nothing you don't already know I'm guessing."

"Take your time. Don't rush anything." Susan smiled at him.

The next couple days he spent a lot of time texting Oscar back and forth.

Chapter Ten

"You seem very happy." Stan smiled at Trey as he was driving him home.

"I am. It's funny how things work out." Trey smiled as he looked at his phone.

"Don't put all your eggs in one basket." Stan smiled as he just kept looking forward.

"What do you mean?"

"I mean, my boss said his son tends to jump from guy to guy. Things get going and he freaks out and runs."

The happiness left him for a moment. "Maybe the other guys just moved to fast." Tray suggested and sighed.

"That is a good possibility. So, take your time."

"I will."

"What I told you is between us. I don't need problems with my boss for giving me a heads up."

"I understand."

"Looks like dad is out in the fields already." Stand pointed as they pulled in the drive way.

"Thank you for everything." Trey smiled at him.

"Give me a hug." Stan leaned over and hugged him. "I love you and don't want to see you hurt anymore."

"I know."

"Tell mom I had to go. I have to get back. Things to do."

"You don't want a million questions."

"That to." Stan put his finger to his lips to tell him to be quiet about that.

Trey closed the door and headed into the house.

"OK, first let me say how sorry I am for listening to Clayton. I thought he knew this guy better." His mom said as she offered him some cake.

"It's fine." Trey laughed and sat down at the table.

"Where is Stan?" His mother looked around.

"He said he is sorry, but he had to get back."

"Oh, OK. It's just I don't get to see him much." She looked out the window.

Trey was eating the cake and took a drink of the milk she had sat in front of him.

"So, I hear you are talking to a young man?" She looked back at him.

"Yes, he is very nice." He said as he finished and wiped his mouth with the napkin.

"He is nice?" She looked at him wanting more.

"Very nice." He smiled at her as he put his dishes in the sink.

"So, when do I get to meet this very nice young man?"

"I don't know. We are just talking right now. Nothing serious."

"The smile on your face says you are lying." She folded her arms.

"I am excited that there may be more. I am very attracted to him."

"I see."

"I'm going to put my stuff away and go help dad."

"Clayton is with him yet today."

"OK. I just want to catch up with them."

She watched him as he got to the stairs and he looked back to see her pull out her phone. He laughed to himself knowing she was calling Stan. He wasn't getting out of the million questions that easy.

A short time later he was walking out of the house. He could hear his mother talking to Stan, and he laughed to himself. He walked out to the barn where Clayton and his dad were taking a break.

"Well, look who has decided to come home." Clayton smiled at him.

"You're an ass. That guy was awful." Trey said as he playfully punched his arm.

"I'm sorry about that."

"You should be." His dad said before Trey could respond. "I told both of them to stay out of your life. You will find someone when the time is right." His dad shook his head and grabbed his right arm.

"Are you ok?" Trey looked concerned.

"He pulled it fighting with the bailer this morning." Clayton shook his head.

"I fixed it didn't I."

"I told you I would get it."

"Listen the only ones that know how to fix it is me and Trey. You never paid any attention when I would show you things."

"Oh, I'm so glad your home. He has done nothing but say how you know everything and I know nothing."

"Because he paid attention when I taught him things."

Trey was smiling on the inside; his dad missed him.

"I did miss your help son. It's been like a one-man crew with a blind man for assistance."

"I can't wait to get back on the road again. Nice and quiet there." Clayton huffed and turned and headed toward the house.

"Dad, he took time off to be here for you." Trey started.

"I know. He knows I appreciate it." His dad waved his hand toward Clayton, who stopped looked back and shook his head.

"Ok, fine I'll finish helping today." Clayton sighed knowing that was as close to a sorry as he was going to get.

"Are we done being girls now. We have a lot of work to do, this damned bailer set us back again." His dad looked at Trey to see if he hurt his feelings with that comment.

"Let me have a look." Trey said as he stepped in front of his dad, and in a few minutes he had it working.

"How the hell did you do that?" Clayton was aggravated. "I was working on it all morning."

"Because he pays attention to me." His dad patted him on the back and walked toward the tractor.

"You're a show off."

Trey shrugged his shoulders then heard his dad yell. They both looked up in time to see him fall by the tractor.

Chapter Eleven

Trey and his brothers sat in the ER waiting room. His mother had been back with their dad for over an hour. They had said nothing to each other, all lost in their own thoughts.

"Mom." Clayton said as she walked into the waiting room. Tears in her eyes.

"What happen?" Trey asked.

"He had a massive stroke. He is in bad shape." She lifted her head and they could see she had been crying for a while. The four of them surrounded her and hugged her.

"Anything you need us to do we will do." Stan said as they continued to hold the hug.

"Trey, I need you to run the farm. If you boys can help him in any way."

"It's done mom." Eddie said.

"I don't know what's going to happen boys. He may need a lot of therapy."

"We got your back mom." Trey said.

"They are moving him to a room. I'm staying, but you boys don't have to." She sighed and tried to fight back tears.

The boys just looked at each other.

"We will take turns being here with you mom and taking care of the farm."

"Trey, you stay for now, the rest of us will go pack somethings to stay at the house and be back." Stan said.

They each kissed their mother and headed out.

"They said to wait here and they come get me when he is in a room." She said as she sat down beside Trey.

They said there quiet for a few moments.

"You know your father loves you no matter what?"

"I know."

"He always said you were his farm boy."

Trey smiled at her.

"He said the other boys never had any interest in learning how to run the farm, but you, you picked it up very easy. A natural he would say." She smiled at him.

"He's going to be ok."

She put her hand on his cheeck and tried to smile. "Oh honey, I hope you're right, but I saw him and he doesn't look good." Tears flowed now.

"It just happened mom, he's not going to look good."

"I'm scared." She pulled him in and hugged him.

"We are all here for you mom. We will get through this."

"Excuse me, your husband is in his room. Take the elevator to the 6th floor. Room 612." A nurse smiled at her.

"You go ahead mom. I'm going to go check on things at home and I'll be back with something for you to eat later."

"Honey, I'm not hungry." She smiled as she stood.

"You still have to eat. Don't need you getting sick to."

"It's not fair when your children use your own words against you." She smiled a little at him.

"I love you mom." He hugged her and walked her to the elevator. When the doors closed, he headed to his car. He was almost there when he heard a voice behind him.

"Are you Trey?" He turned to see a skinny little boy standing there with his hands on his hip. His hair was pink, and he had makeup on. The only way Trey knew it was a boy for sure was the Adams apple.

"Yes, what can I do for you?"

The boy walked up and slapped him across the face, catching Trey off guard. Trey pulled back to hit him and stopped himself.

"Stay away from my man you Mr. Green jeans want to be."

"What the hell are you talking about?" Trey's face was still stinging from the slap.

"Oscar is my man. You got it. Old McDonald. Just go back to your farm and play with your sheep and leave him alone."

"Listen boy, I don't know who you are and the only...."

"Did you just assume my gender?" He pulled back to slap him again, and Trey grabbed his arm.

"Listen he, she, they, it or shit stain whatever you are identifying as today. I let the first slap go and didn't lay you out, because my mom is under enough stress with my dad clinging to life in there, but you don't get a second one." He let his hand go and the boy stepped back.

"Randy what are you doing here?" Oscar yelled as he ran over to them.

"Yes, how did you know where to find me."

"Well, we were at lunch and he was texting you. Said he had to meet you, laid his phone down and went to the bathroom. So, I looked."

"You looked in my phone?"

"Well, I have to keep tabs on you. You're sneaking around with Elmer Fud over here playing let's plant something and see what comes up."

"Why didn't you tell me you had a boyfriend?" Trey looked confused.

"Because I don't. We went on one date and I told you that I wasn't into you. Today you just happen to run into me at lunch time when I was almost done eating and just sat down with me. I can't believe you looked at my phone. I told you we could be friends, but after this I don't want anything to do with you."

"You little bastard." Randy said as he pulled back to slap him. Trey grabbed his arm again.

"Try that again and you will need to visit the er for a cast." Trey looked at him leaving no doubt he was serious.

"Well, I hope you will be happy with the Brawny man over there." He spat at Oscar.

"OK, I have seen enough." Came the voice of a security guard as he walked up to the three.

"Yes, they have been committing a hate crime against me." Randy started to point at the two of them.

"No, from what I saw you are the problem. You hit this young man once and tried a second time, and then you tried to hit this other young man. Would you like to press assault charges?" The guard looked at Trey.

"No."

"You're lucky had it been me, you would be in jail. You need to leave this property or I will have you arrested." The officer said to Randy, who looked at the three of them and huffed and walked off.

"Thank you." Trey smiled at the guard.

"Not a problem. You two have a good day." He smiled at the two of them and walked off.

"How is your dad?"

"I'm headed back to the farm. Follow me and we will talk there." They hugged and went to their cars.

Chapter Twelve

Trey and Oscar were sitting at the kitchen table drinking coffee.

"How did you meet that guy?" Trey asked as he stirred his coffee.

"Online. His profile pic looked normal. From the time we met up I was sure I was being pranked, but no that was him."

They both laughed.

"Listen I don't mean to cut things short, but I have a lot of work to get done, and I'm really behind."

"I'll help."

"Really?"

"I don't know much, so you'll have to teach me."

"I can do that. Let's go."

They walked out on the porch as an old crown Victorian pulled up.

"Aunt Ruth." Trey smiled and headed to her car.

"HI honey, how are things going." She asked as she got out of the car.

"Mom is still at the hospital. Dad is in rough shape. They just moved him to a room. Let me take your bag." He took her bag and headed to the porch.

"Who is this handsome young man?"

"Aunt Ruth, this is Oscar."

"Nice to meet you ma'am"

"And polite. Keep this one." She smiled at him.

They were almost to the door when a van pulled up.

"Who the heck..." Trey looked and then couldn't believe his eyes.

"OK, we are here to help. Whatever you need." Alice said as she got out of the passenger seat.

"Who is this?" Ruth started and then smiled. "Carl, James so nice to see you again." Ruth headed over to them.

"Ruth this is my mom, Alice." Carl smiled at her.

"Ruth, from the boat?" Alice looked at Carl, who rolled his eyes and nodded.

"Pleasure to meet you." Ruth smiled.

"Pleasure is all mine. Now my boys are here to do whatever needs done." Alice smiled.

"What do you all know about farming?" Trey asked as he walked over.

"Nothing." Carl smiled.

"She made us watch YouTube videos on farming on the way here." Arron moaned.

"Learning something new never hurt anyone, now get the food out of the back and take it into the kitchen."

Trey looked as the driver got out of the van and saw Benton closing the door. He smiled big and lit up.

"So that's how you knew where I lived." Trey smiled and went over and hugged Benton.

"OK, so let's go figure out what everyone needs to do." They all headed inside.

Oscar grabbed Trey's arm as he walked by and stopped him.

"Who are all these people?"

"Oh my God. I didn't mean to be so rude. I will introduce you when we get inside."

"Can we talk?"

"Sure."

"Who was the driver?"

"That's Benton a good friend of mine."

"Good friend?"

"Yeah, why."

Oscar just looked at him.

"Listen there is nothing going on with us. I wanted to but he isn't interested."

"Didn't look that way."

"His husband passed away not long ago; he doesn't want to be in a relationship right now."

"Right now?"

"Listen I was just happy to see him is all."

"I could see that. Happier to see him than any of the others."

"I don't know what you want me to tell you."

"If we were both available right now, who would you choose?"

"What?"

"Listen I think you are a nice guy, who I would love to date."

"I feel the same way."

"But I don't want to be a second choice."

"You wouldn't be."

"I would be right now. You still have strong feelings for him."

"What do you want me to say?" Trey was tearing up now.

"Nothing, you know I'm right." He stepped in and hugged Trey.

"When you're over him, call then. If I'm single maybe we can look at dating then."

"But."

"No, buts. I'm going to go now. Seems you have a lot of help."

"Can we still be friends?"

"Of course, but give me some time right now. I'm a little hurt right now."

"I didn't mean…."

"I know, I'm glad this happened now. We can still work on a friendship. Later that might not have been possible." He blew him a kiss and walked to his car.

Trey took a deep breath and tried to pull himself together.

"He isn't the only one who noticed how you lit up when you saw Benton." Ruth's voice came from behind him. He turned and smiled.

"I don't know what to do."

"You'll figure it out. If the journey were easy, it wouldn't be as fun." She put her arm around him and walked toward the house.

"Fun?"

"Yeah, come help. That Alice, she is a take charge kind of gal."

"I know."

"She is my kind of gal." Ruth giggled.

Trey just lowered his head and shook it.

Chapter Thirteen

Stan, Sandy and Eddie had shown up as everyone headed out to the barn to get started. Now Sandy, Ruth and Alice stood on the front porch and looked at the mess walking toward them.

"What are you doing?" Ruth looked at Sandy.

"Oh, I have to get pictures of this." She laughed as she held her phone up.

"Can you send them to me then?" Alice laughed.

"Sure."

"Hey Arron did you have a rough time?" Alice called to him as he headed toward the house.

"I am not a farmer!" He yelled as he kept brushing at his clothes.

"What exactly were you doing?" Ruth asked.

"Cleaning the pens. I kept falling into actual shit. Who the hell wants to do this for a living?"

"There is an outside shower around the back. I'll see what clothes the boys have there that might fit." Ruth pointed.

Arron shook his head and headed to where she pointed.

"Hey James."

"Don't even. I'm still legally blind you know." He held up his hand.

"I told him not to lean so far over." Eddie said as he followed him.

"Lean over?" Alice was confused.

"All he had to do was put food in for the pigs." Eddie said.

"That bag was heavy." James moaned.

"I told you to use the scoop, but you said no it would be faster to just dump it out of the bag."

"Again I know."

"What happen?" Sandy asked as she snapped pictures.

"He went right over the top with the bag. He tried to get out but the pigs were hungry and ended up knocking him into the water." Eddie tried not to laugh.

"He was no help at all."

"Shower out back, Eddie, go see what clothes you can find for him and Arron." Ruth pointed, and they did as they were told.

"This is better than tv." Alice laughed.

"Here comes Antonio with a bucket and wet." Alice shook her head.

"YouTube makes milking a cow look much easier than it is." Antonio sighed.

"I did just fine." Stan walked behind him with a full bucket."

"Show off." Antonio turned his bucket upside down and nothing was in it."

"Where is your milk?" Ruth asked knowing the answer.

Antonio just swung his arms wide in front of him displaying his wet clothes.

"She kept kicking his bucket. It was so funny." Stan tried to make it look like he wasn't laughing.

"Some teacher you are." Antonio kicked his bucket across the yard.

"Shower out back, Stan, see if there is anything here that might fit him."

"Well here come the last of them."

Carl and Benton were covered in dirt and hay.

"What happened guys?" Sandy asked as again she was snapping pictures.

"I showed them how to stack the hay on the wagon." Trey shook his head.

"I tried Carl didn't..." Benton started.

"I told you it was right." Carl cut him off.

"They were putting the last bails on the wagon and it all fell off, along with them. They all rolled down the hill. Lucky, they ended right by the barn." Trey smiled.

"Shower around the corner. Your brothers are already looking for clothes for the others."

Clayton and their mother showed up as everyone got ready to sit down to eat. They were all glad to hear that their dad was doing well. They recounted what had happen and their mother laughed for the first time in a couple of days.

After dinner Trey went outside and sat on the porch.

"What are you thinking?" Benton came and sat down beside him.

"Worried about my dad, thinking this is going to be mine to run one day." Trey said without looking at him.

"Is that what you want?"

"It's all I know."

"I didn't ask that."

"You know what I really want?"

"What?"

"To find someone to spend the rest of my life with, someone to run this place with me."

"You will find him someday."

"I have a question for you." Trey still didn't look at him.

"I'm not a farmer, I think today proved that."

"No," Trey half laughed. "Do you ever think about what happen in school?"

"The locker room, yes."

"I just want you to know I'm sorry. I didn't really want to treat you like that, but I just went along with the guys."

"I know."

"That's not a good excuse, I know. It's the only one I have though."

"Why are you telling me this?"

"My brother set me up with a guy, who was not nice to me to say the least. I didn't like how I felt, and if I ever made you feel that way, I'm very sorry. It was awful."

"Can I tell you something?" Benton smiled at him.

"What?" He finally looked at him.

"I liked it."

"You what?"

"I like being treated ruff. In the bedroom I mean. It turns me on."

"Really?"

"I like it soft and sweet to, It all has it's place."

"I don't think I could be like that with someone I care about." Trey sighed.

"I know." He patted the top of his leg.

"Is that why you don't want to date me?"

"No, well not the main reason. The main reason is I still miss Allen, I've loved him a long time. And even though sex is not everything, it's important and we are not a match there. It would end up bad. I don't want that because I care to much about you."

"I see." Trey seemed broken hearted.

"Would you rather me lie to you?"

"No." They were both sanding now.

"You're like a brother to me. I'll always be here for you."

"Thank you." Trey stepped in for a hug, and Benton grabbed him pulling him in and hugging him tightly.

"I'm glad your in my life."

"But I'm not a farmer."

"None of you are." Trey laughed.

Trey and his family thanked everyone for all their help as they left. Exhausted the family was soon off to bed.

"Trey honey, the hospital called we need to go now." His mother woke him just after two a.m.

Chapter Fourteen

Later that morning they were all sitting in a small office. His mother had visited with their dad and reported he did not look good. Stan sat in the chair beside his mother holding her hand as Trey and his brothers stood behind them.

"Sorry to keep you waiting." The doctor said as he came in closing the door behind him. He sat down and looked over the group in front of him.

"What happen?" Stan finally asked.

"He had a massive stroke around one thirty this morning. It's very luck he was here, had he been at home he most likely would not be with us." The doctor stopped to let what he said sink in.

"How is he now?" Trey asked fighting back tears.

"He is stable, but we are not sure the extent of the damage."

"Damage?" Stan asked as his mother tighten her grip on his hand.

"There is going to be damage, he may not have use of certain parts of his body. He will need a lot of therapy."

They were all quiet, just looking at each other. Their mother started softly crying.

"He is still not awake, but you can visit him one at a time. He will know you're there even if he doesn't respond. I will let you know more information as it becomes available. I'm sorry, I wish I had better news."

"Thank you doctor." Stan stood with his mother, as the doctor shook all their hands.

"You may sit here as long as you need." The doctor said and left.

"I want to go to him." Anna said.

"I'm going back home, there is a lot of work to do." Trey said as he hugged his mother.

"I will call you when we hear something." Stan said.

"Ok." He left as his brothers were talking, he didn't really hear anything they said. His mind was racing.

A short time later he was home feeding the animals and cleaning stalls.

"Do you need a hand?" A voice came from behind him. He turned to see Benton standing there. He looked a him half smileing, took a deep breath and tears started rolling down his face.

"I'm not..." Trey couldn't say anything else. Benton walked over and hugged him.

"I'm here for you buddy." He hugged him tightly.

Trey pulled back and pulled himself together.

"It's not good." Trey said looking down at the ground.

"My aunt sent food."

"I'm not really hungry."

"Want to help me take it into the house?"

Trey just looked at him.

"She sent to boxes full of containers with food."

"Yeah, I'll help."

They walked over to the van in silence. They each took a box and went into the kitchen. They put the food away, and Trey made a coffee and they sat at the table.

"I don't know what to do." Trey finally said.

"Can I help?"

"I need help here. I can't do everything." Trey sighed.

"I'm not much help there, but I'll do what I can."

"I would love to have you help, but." Trey stopped and half smiled.

"But what?" Benton asked already kind of knowing what he was going to say.

"You know how I feel about you. I have a lot going on and I don't know..."

"I know, it's ok. I'm your friend."

"I know."

The door opened it was his mother and Stan.

"How is he?" Trey asked.

"No change. I brought mom home to get cleaned up and maybe eat something."

"Honey I'm not hungry."

"Mom, you need to eat, we don't need you to get sick." Trey said as he hugged her.

"My aunt sent a bunch of food. It's in the fridg."

"She is so sweet." Trey's mom said "I'm going to get a shower first."

They watched her go upstairs, as his other brothers came into the house.

"We have to talk." Stan said to them as they sat down.

"This seems like family stuff. I should be going." Benton stood.

"Tell your aunt thank you for all the food." Trey smiled at him.

"Can you just wait a few minutes outside?" Stan said and Trey looked confused.

"Yeah." Benton answered just as confused.

Benton walked out and sat on the swing, and the four brothers just looked at each other.

"OK, you three seem to know something I don't." Trey said looking at each of their faces.

"Dad is in really bad shape. He isn't responding to anything." Clayton started to say.

"What do you mean?" Trey asked not sure he wanted to know.

"The doctors think he may not have use of his legs and maybe his arms." Eddie said tears forming.

"What?" Trey couldn't believe his ears.

"They have run test and he isn't responding to them." Eddie continued.

"There is more." Stan sighed.

"More?"

"Several years ago, dad cut back on the health insurance. He just couldn't afford it anymore."

Trey just looked at them not sure he wanted to hear anymore.

"He is going to need to go to a nursing home. It's going to be very expensive." Clayton grabbed his hand.

"Can we just bring him home?"

"Mom can't take care of him in this shape, and full-time nurses would be even more expensive." Stan said.

"Then the insurance will cover the nursing home?" Trey looked at them and none of them could look him in the face.

"Mom couldn't bear to tell you; she knows how much you love the farm." Eddie had tears flowing now.

"We have to sell the farm Trey, it's the only way." Stan said trying not to cry himself.

"But where will mom go?"

"She is going to live with me for now. Eddie is going to stay at school. You and Clayton can stay at the trailer." Stan finished.

"Won't that have to be sold?"

"That is in my name. I bought it for dad, but he would never put it in his name." Stan told him.

"What am... I don't..." Trey couldn't even put a thought together. He just got up and went out on the porch. Benton was sitting and had heard everything. Trey stopped and looked at him and broke down. Benton grabbed him and they sat down on the steps.

"This is my fault." Trey started. His brothers were at the door listening now.

"How do you figure that?" Benton asked.

"I came out. This is God punishing the family." Trey sobbed.

"God doesn't work that way." Benton put his arm around him.

"I don't know why else all this would be happening."

"We don't blame you at all." Stan said as he came out.

"I need to get out of here." Trey looked back at his brothers who were crying now.

"Trey, we love you. You did nothing wrong." Eddie said.

"Trey honey, your father never looked after his health. He just kept pushing off taking care of himself, because of this or that." His mother said as she pushed passed his brothers.

"Mom, I'm so sorry."

"You have nothing to be sorry for. You have been the backbone of this farm for several years now. I'm sorry that things are going the way they are."

They all slowly group hugged as Benton watched on.

"Why don't you stay with your friend tonight. I'm going back to the hospital. I will call if anything changes." His mother wiped a tears from his eyes with her thumps. "Clayton is taking a short run; Eddie is going back to school and Stan has to go home. I don't want you to be alone."

"I'll stay with you." Trey offered.

"They will only let me stay. I'll be fine. Now go with your friend."

Trey looked at Benton, who nodded he could come.

Chapter Fifteen

"Thanks for letting me stay." Trey said as he followed Benton into his house.

"You could have ridden with me."

"I just wanted my own car, in case I had to leave quick."

"I understand."

They sat at the table with just the light above the sink on.

"I don't know what I'm going to do?" Trey finally said.

"You'll figure it out."

"My whole life is gone in the matter of a couple of days."

"I know how that feels." Benton half smiled.

"How did you make it through it all?"

"Lots of support from family and friends."

"Thanks for being my friend."

"Always. Why don't you try and get some rest."

"I think I just want to set here a while."

"Spare room second door on the left." He smiled and walked upstairs.

Benton came down in the morning to find Trey asleep with his head on the table.

"Hey, Trey." He said softly as he started to make a pot of coffee.

"Huh, what?" Trey lifted his head and moaned in pain.

"A little stiff?" Benton smiled at him.

"I guess I dozed off."

"I'm making coffee."

"Good."

"Why don't you go take a shower."

"Yeah, that might be a good idea." He grabbed his bag and headed upstairs. A short time later he was back down.

"Your coffee is on the table."

"Thank you."

"Listen, I am going to my cousins house, we are cooking out for lunch."

"I'll pass. Not really into seeing people. I'll just go back to the farm."

"Your brother got someone to come take care of the animals for now."

"Then maybe I'll just crash here if that is, ok?"

"It is, but you know Alice is only going to make someone come get you."

"Ok, fine. I'm driving myself, that way if something happens, I can go."

"That works."

A short time later they were pulling into Carl's place.

"Well, isn't this a nice surprise." Alice said as she hugged Trey.

"Nice to see you, thank you for all the food you sent."

"Well, you need to eat." She smiled at him.

Everyone else said hi, and he could feel all of them pitying him, and it made him uncomfortable.

"Listen I need a little time alone." Trey said to Benton after a while.

"The food is almost ready."

"I won't be long and I'm not really hungry."

"OK." Benton agreed, but not happy about it.

Trey walked out and could hear Alice asking where he was going. He got in his car and his phone went off; it was Benton. He smiled and didn't answer it, not wanting to listen to Alice lecture him. He drove up the Freeland Mountain, past the Freeland diner and drove around town listening to music, he found himself setting at a stop sign looking at a small church. He sighed looking at the church and pulled into the small empty parking lot across from it. He slowly walked over to the church and tried the door and it was locked. He looked at the sign and it said Bethal Baptist. He turned and sat on the step.

"God, I don't know if you are listening or not. If you are mad at me, I'm sorry but please don't take it out on my dad. He is a good guy." He stopped speaking and put his face in his hands, tears flowed as he cried. He just sat there like that hoping for some kind of answer that he knew wasn't coming.

"Are you OK sir?" Trey heard as he felt a hand touch his shoulder. He jumped to see a man not much older than him, smiling at him. He was slender and dressed well.

"Yes, sorry." Trey started to get up, wiping his eyes.

"There is nothing to be sorry for. Do you need help?"

"I just thought I should talk to God and this seemed the place to do it."

"Well, you don't need to be at church to talk to God, but maybe he led you here for a reason." They both sat down. "I'm Jeremy." He reached out his hand.

"I'm Trey." He shook his hand back.

"Well, Trey what seems to be the problem, what brought you here."

"You don't want to know."

"I'm a good listener."

"I was kind of hoping to talk to the pastor."

"You're in luck. I'm the guy."

"You?"

"Yes, sir."

He looked at Jeremy for a moment and sighed.

"I think God is mad at me and is taking it out on my dad."

"I see, what happen to make you believe this?"

"I came out to my family a short time ago, and now my dad had a massive stroke and we have to sell the farm because the insurance isn't going to cover his nursing home cost."

"Do you really believe that God works that way?"

He looked at Jeremy for a moment to see if he could see the right answer in his face.

"I don't know, does he?"

"No. God loves you no matter what."

"Even if what I'm attracted to makes me a sinner."

"First, we all sin. Every single one of us."

"OK"

"Do you believe God makes mistakes?"

"I'm going to go with no."

"No, he doesn't. He loves you the way you are."

"So, it's not my fault."

"No, I don't believe it is.

"So why is everything happening then?"

"I'm afraid I don't have the answer to that, but I do know that our faith will be tested. The best we can do is look toward God and ask for direction."

"I don't know if I know how to do that." Trey hung his head.

"Well, something brought you here, that's a good start."

"Where do I start?" Trey looked up at him.

"Do you want me to pray with you?"

"Would you?"

"Yes, of course." He took Trey's hand and bowed his head and Trey followed.

"Dear, Lord my brother Trey needs your guidance. He and his family are going through a tuff time right now and they need your light to shine on them, to comfort them in these ruff times. Dear Lord look after his father as he struggles with his health issues. Please Lord bring peace to the family, and may you watch over my new friend Trey as he struggles to find peace with who he is. In God's name we pray Amen."

"Amen." Trey added.

"Are you feeling better?" Jeremy smiled at him as they both stood.

"Yeah, some. Thank you so much."

"Anytime."

Trey started walking to his car and turned back.

"How did you know I was here?" Trey looked confused.

"My wife seen you on the security camera, she called me said that you looked like you were in distress. I was only a couple of blocks away."

"Wow that was lucky." Trey smiled.

"God works in mysterious ways." Jeremy smiled and waved to him as he got in his car.

Chapter Sixteen

A week later, Trey was packing the things in his room into a box. He looked at the trophies from the Future Farmers of America.

"Lot of good these do me now." He put them in the box and started pulling boxes out from under the bed. He finished packing them and then finished with his clothes. He slowly took them out to his truck. He looked around. The animals had been sold the day before. The life he had thought he knew was gone. He put the last box in the back of the truck and shut the tail gate.

"Are you doing, OK?" Stan asked as he walked from the barn.

"I don't know, I'm not sure what my life is now." He just stared at the house.

"Did you get everything?"

"I think so. I'm going to go check one more time." He started to walk toward the house, as two cars pulled up. It was his mom and brothers.

"How are you mom?" Trey asked as he hugged her.

"As good as I can be." She fought back tears.

"The movers are coming next week." Eddie said.

"At least mom can stay with dad at the nursing home." Clayton added.

"I'm going to check to see if I got everything out of my room." Trey sighed and headed into the house, before he started crying. His mother's face was breaking his heart.

Trey looked around his room and sat on the bed and put his head into his hands. After a few minutes he took a deep breath and started to stand and the bed slid and hit the wall, and a floor board popped lose. He picked it up and, in the floor, there was a cigar box covered in dust. He pulled it out and opened it slowly. There were some old baseball cards wrapped in a rubber band and black and white picture of two boys. One maybe ten and the other five he thought. Some letters that were faded and hard to read, but he thought they were love letters.

"Are you OK?" Stan yelled up the stairs.

"Yes, I'm coming down." He put everything back in the box and headed down stairs.

"Honey, do you want any dishes, or anything for the kitchen?"

"No, but ..."

"Are you sure, because I don't know what I'm going to do with all this."

"Mom, look what I found under the floor board by my bed." He set the cigar box on the table.

"Oh wow." Clayton looked as Trey opened it.

"Who is in the pic mom?" Trey asked as he held it up.

"The little one is your father, and the other." She stopped. "I don't know, probably doesn't matter. Just throw it away,"

"You do know." Stan said as they all looked at her waiting for an answer.

"Well, I guess it won't hurt if you know now."

"Know what?" Stan cocked his head.

"That is your dad's older brother. I don't recall his name, but him and your grandfather had a falling out when he was seventeen or eighteen. He left and never showed his face around here again."

"What did they fight over?" Eddie asked.

"Yeah, like what could be so bad?" Clayton added.

"His dad wouldn't tell anyone and he didn't come back around for anyone to ask him."

"Do you think he is still alive?" Trey asked.

"Don't know. I never met him. I was just told about him. I know your dad's heart was broke. He looked up to him."

"Can I keep this stuff?" Trey asked.

"Finders keepers." His mom smiled at him. "Now what about the furniture in the living room. Any of you need that?" She said as she went through more dishes, and packed what she wanted to take with her.

"Mom, the movers are coming next week. They will pack everything and get it to where it needs to be." Stan grabbed her shoulders.

"I know I just need to be doing something." She hung her head.

"Go home with Stan get some rest. We will meet you here in the morning." Clayton said.

She looked at all of them and they were just as tired as she was.

"OK, fine." They all grabbed a few things and headed out.

Trey sat on his porch looking at the picture again with the cigar box sitting beside him. A car pulled up and he lifted his head.

"Hey I just wanted to check on you." Benton said as he got out of his car.

"I'm fine, but you're not going to believe what I found today."

"Why, what?" Benton was standing in front of him.

"Look at this pic. I found it in a cigar box hidden in the floor board of my bedroom.

"Who is it?"

"The younger one is my dad, the older is his brother."

"I didn't know he had a brother."

"Neither did we. Mom said that him and his dad had a fight and he never came around again."

"Oh, my God." Benton looked at the pic again and his eyes got wide.

"What's his brothers name?"

"No one knows."

"Would you believe I think I know who this is?"

"Really?"

"Yeah."

"Is he still alive?"

"Very much so."

"Can we go see him."

"Yes."

Chapter Seventeen

Two days later Trey was sitting in Benton's kitchen.

"Are you sure he is coming?" Trey sat nervous.

"Yeah, and maybe, you had enough coffee." Benton smiled as he watched him shake.

"I'm just nervous is all. I should have told the others."

"We are not sure we are right. Let's make sure first."

A knock came at the door, and Trey almost jumped out of his seat.

"Relax." Benton motioned with his hand for him to sit. Benton went to the door.

"Benton. What's up?"

"Chris thanks for coming." Benton smiled as he motioned for him to sit.

"Hi I'm Chris." He held out his hand to Trey, who was shocked at how much he looked like the young man in the picture.

"This is Trey." Benton said clearing his throat, bringing Trey back.

"Yes, sorry, nice to meet you." He shook his hand.

"Chris would you like coffee?" Benton asked as he sat down.

"Yes, So, what did you need to talk to me about?"

Benton sat the coffee on the table and looked at Trey. Trey took the Cigar box from his lap and sat it on the table, and Chris's face went pale.

"Where did you get this?" Chris asked fighting the urge to grab it.

"It was under the floor board in my bedroom." Trey looked at him.

"Interesting." Chris looked at Trey and half smiled.

"Do you recognize it?" Benton asked already knowing the answer.

Chris reached out and opened it slowly, tears coming to his face.

"It has been a long time." He took the picture out and studied it.

"So, that's you in the picture?" Trey asked.

"Yes." He sighed.

"So, you're my uncle." Trey smiled.

"Excuse me?" Chris lowered the picture and looked at Trey who had tears in his eyes.

"That's my dad in the picture with you."

"Your dad?"

"He had a massive stroke. He is in a nursing home and we have to sell the farm. I was moving things out of my room and came across the lose board under the bed."

"Oh." Chris just looked at him trying to take in everything he was hearing.

"What happened?" Benton asked.

"It's a long story." Chris sighed.

"We got time. I'll make more coffee." Benton said.

"My dad never knew why. He looked up to you and when you left his heart was broke."

"Remember the day of the car accident and I said that Dillan was with me instead of his cousin." Chris started.

"Yes." Benton smiled.

"Well, there is more to that story."

"Go on." Trey said not really understanding anything so far.

"We were supposed to go out that night, but he had stopped by the farm earlier that day to tell me that plans had changed. We were down behind the barn talking and I said I was going to miss him, but I understood." Chris looked at Trey for a moment.

"Trey came out a short time ago. It's ok." Benton reassured Chris.

"Really?"

"Yeah. Please continue."

"Well. Before he left, I grabbed him an planted a big kiss that I held for too long."

"What do you mean?"

"I got lost in it and didn't hear my dad come around the corner of the barn. All I heard was what the hell is going on."

"Oh shit." Benton said without thinking.

"Well Dillan ran and my dad never realized who it was, He asked me repeatedly, but I wouldn't tell."

"That was the big fight." Trey sighed.

"He said I was no longer a part of the family if that was the life I was going to lead. I told him fine. We screamed at each other for a few minutes and I went to my room and pack my clothes."

"You left and never came back." Trey shook his head.

"Well on my way out, dad stopped me. He told me that if I ever told anyone what I was he would make sure I would regret it. He knew where coal pits were. He was not going to be known for having a faggot as a son."

"Oh, my God." Benton blurted again.

"I left and found Dillon, who was helping me find somewhere to stay instead of being with his cousin. After the accident I drifted around for a while avoiding family anytime, I seen them out. Fearing dad would go through with his promise."

"After he died why didn't you come around?" Trey was almost in tears.

"By then I was secure in who I was, had my own place and a good job. I didn't want to go through that emotional coaster again."

"This is unbelievable." Trey shook his head.

"It's a small world."

"Oh my God." Chris took the letters out of the box.

"What?" Trey asked wiping tears.

"These are the letters I wrote to Dillan telling him how much I loved him. I never had the nerve to give them to him back then." He pulled them in and held them tight against his chest.

"I think you should go see my dad." Trey smiled.

"I don't know."

"Let's go to the farm, I think everyone is there packing the last of the things up."

Chris looked at Benton, who smiled and nodded.

"It's time you reunite with your family."

Chapter Eighteen

Benton drove, Chris sat up front and Trey in the back. As they pulled in Chris started to tear up.

"Oh my God it's been so long." He tried to hold back the emotions that were about to overflow.

"Are you OK?" Trey put his hand on his shoulder.

"I'll be fine." He patted his hand and Trey left go and sat back.

As they got out of the car Aunt Ruth was on the porch.

"It's Aunt Ruth." Chris said more to himself than anyone else.

Ruth stared for a moment then her eyes grew as she realized who was walking toward her.

"As I live and breathe. Chris!" She darted off the porch and gave him a huge hug. Seeing Ruth run made everyone else come out of the house.

"Aunt Ruth it is so good to see you." Chris couldn't hold the tears back anymore.

"I didn't think I'd ever see you again. Your father made it clear you would never be back."

"I know."

"But he never said why." She was now wiping her own tears.

"Who is this?" Stan asked as they all looked confused.

"This is Chris. Your father's brother." Ruth turned and smiled at them.

They all stood in shock and then looked at Benton and Trey.

"How did you find him?" Anna asked shaking her head.

"Turns out Benton knew him and recognized him in the picture."

"This is a blessing for sure." Ruth took him by the hand, as they all headed back into the house.

They all sat and listened as Chris recounted what had happen and why he never came around.

"Your Father was always a bit of a hot head." Ruth looked sad. "I wish you had come stayed with us."

"In those days would you have been understanding?" Chris looked at her.

"Probably not." It hurt Ruth to admit.

"Well thank God Trey found my box." Chris opened it. "This pic is from Ben's first day of school. He was so excited to go on the bus with his big brother."

"Wow it looks like you have some old cards there." Eddie eyed them up.

"You can look at them if you like." Chris handed them to him. "I actually forgot I had them in there."

Eddie took them and as he looked through them his eyes got wide.

"Do you realize what you have here?" He broke into the conversation that was going on.

"What do you mean?" Chris looked over.

"A Mike Schmitt rookie card, a seventy-three Roberto Clemente a seventy and seventy-five Nolan Ryan, to name just a couple."

"So." His mother said.

"These are worth thousands of dollars. They are all in mint condition."

"You're kidding?" Chris said as Eddie handed them back to him.

They all looked at each other for a few minutes, then Chris looked at Trey.

"I want you to have these, you can buy the farm."

"I couldn't."

"You were supposed to get the farm. Let me make that happen for you."

Trey looked around at everyone and they all had tears in their eyes.

"Take them." Clayton urged him.

"But everything is already sold. How would I run it." Trey said in a trembling voice.

"If anyone can do it, it is you." Stan said smiling at him.

Trey looked at Chris.

"Please take them. You found them and gave me back my family."

"But..."

"This farm has been in this family for four generations; I don't want to see it end now. Take the cards." Chris took Trey's hands and put the cards in them. "Just as long as I am able to visit."

"Anytime you want to." Trey said still in shock.

"I think I'd like to see my old room if that's OK." Chris stood.

"Yes, please." Trey smiled

"I'll call the realtor and tell him we have a buyer; we don't need him." His mother smiled for the first time in weeks.

"Let's unpack the kitchen." Ruth stood.

"The coffee pot first please." Clayton went right for that box.

Trey turned and went upstairs and found Chris sitting on the bed.

"May I come in?" Trey said softly.

"Please do." Chris looked back and smiled at him.

"I don't know how to thank you." Trey said as he sat down on the bed.

"You know when I threw my clothes in the garbage bag that day and left. I didn't think I would ever see this room again." Chris looked around the room as memories flooded his mind.

"You're welcome here when ever." Trey smiled.

"I've lost so much time."

Trey just looked at him not sure what to say, so he just listened.

"For the first month or so I lived out of my old burn orange gremlin. It was so small. I made it work. I went to truck stops and used showers there. I would ask truckers for help to pay for it. Some would some wouldn't. I finally got a job doing landscaping and after a month I rented a bedroom."

Trey just continued to listen unable to think of anything to say.

"For the first couple of years I was sure one day dad would show up and say come home. We love you no matter what. Then one day I heard that he was telling people he didn't know what happen to me and didn't care. I gave up after that."

"But you did well for yourself."

"I'm happy for you. Happy that you can be who you are." Chris looked at him.

"Thank you."

"And proud that you had the courage to do it. It's not easy, even now."

"I think they made coffee I can smell it." Trey smiled.

"I'm happy that I am able to help you keep this farm."

"The whole family is happy."

"I could use a cup of coffee."

"Come on let's go."

Chapter Nineteen

"Good morning." Chris said as he walked into the kitchen, of his childhood home.

"Good morning honey." Anna said as she sat a cup of coffee in front of him. "I'm afraid I don't have much here for breakfast." She pointed to a box of donuts sitting on the table.

"These will be fine." He grabbed a glazed donut, broke it in half and dipped it into his coffee. He took a bite and looked at Anna who had tears in her eyes.

"Are you OK?"

"Yes, it's just that's how Ben always ate his donuts."

"Better than sugar to sweeten your coffee."

Anna smiled. "He would say the same thing."

"Good morning, everyone." Trey walked into the kitchen.

"Where is everyone else?" Chris looked around.

"The boys had work and Ruth left early this morning. She needed to get home. But everyone is coming on Sunday for a picnic. We want you here to." She looked at Chris.

"Wouldn't miss it."

"Dad is going to be so happy to see you." Trey smiled at him.

"I hope so." Chris smiled back.

"He will. Over the years he has talked about you, and hoped one day you would come around." Anna said as she finished her coffee.

"Should we get going then." Chris said as he sat his empty cup in the sink.

"Let's go." Trey jumped up grabbed another donut and sat his cup in the sink.

"Are you coming with me?" Anna asked.

"I'm driving myself. I want to go see if I can sell these cards today." Trey smiled at Chris.

"I'll Ride with Trey if that's ok." Chris smiled at her. "I have work later myself."

"That's fine." Anna smiled.

The drive to the nursing home was about twenty minutes, and Chris was lost in his own thoughts. He remembered how close he and Ben had been. How Ben followed him around like a lost puppy. He remembered the day he left, Ben was sitting on the porch with his mother and he raced out the drive way. He felt bad that he never got to tell him why. He started thinking he should have found a way to let him know, but that was all in the past now.

"We are here." Trey said as he parked the car.

"I have knots in my stomach." Chris smiled at him.

"It's going to be fine."

They got out of the car and followed Anna in.

"Good morning honey." Anna said as she entered Ben's room.

"Good morning." Ben struggled to say.

"I have someone who wants to see you."

Ben looked confused, and Anna motioned for Chris to come in. Bens eyes got wide and tears filled them.

"My brother." Ben slowly said.

"His speech is getting a little better, as is his movement. The therapy is working, but it's going to take time." Anna explained.

"How?" Ben looked at Anna.

Anna stepped aside and pointed to Trey. "He found a box in his floor boards that had this picture in it."

Chris showed him the picture, and Ben smiled.

"Mom thought she lost this." He smiled.

"I took it long before I left. You were so excited that day to be going on the bus with me."

Ben looked at Trey still a little confused.

"My friend Benton recognized Chris and arranged for me to meet him."

"Thank Benton." Ben lifted his hand toward Chris who took it and held it. They both had tears flowing now.

"More good news dear, the farm is saved." Anna smiled at him.

"What?"

"These cards were in the box as well. They are worth a lot of money, and Chris gave them to me so I could buy the farm." Trey showed the cards to his dad.

"Thank you." Ben squeezed his hand slightly.

"The least I could do. I'm sorry for not letting you know what happen."

"I knew."

Everyone looked at each other for a moment.

"Mom and I heard what dad said to you as you left." Ben slowly said.

"You did?"

"We never talked." Ben stopped emotions over taking him now.

"You never said anything to me." Anna was shocked.

"Mom said to never talk about it." Ben looked at her.

"So, is that why you were ok with me?" Trey chimed in.

"Yes. You and Stan."

"Wait you know about Stan?" Anna was shocked.

"I knew for a long time about both. Just never said anything."

Everyone was quiet now, different thoughts running through their heads.

"Trey and I are going to step out and let you two catch up." Anna finally said. She motioned for Trey to follow.

"How did he know?" Trey said as they got outside.

"Well, you didn't hide it well."

"I tried."

"I guess he is more observant than we gave him credit for."

"I mean most people didn't know right."

"They did honey." She took his hand and patted it.

"But I had girlfriends."

"The way you look at people will always give it away."

"What?"

"When you find someone attractive you look at them in a different way, you didn't hide that well at all."

"I'm going to take the cards to a guy I know. Tell Chris to call me when he needs to leave."

"OK, honey. Good luck."

A short time later Trey was at a pawn shop. The owner and him were friends, so he hoped he would be able to help.

"Well good to see you. What brings you by." A tall slender man with black hair and brown eyes stood behind a counter. He was a couple years older than Trey, but they knew each other from high school, and hung out with the same crowd.

"Hey, Peter I have a question for you."

"Sure, glad to help."

"Where can I sell these?" He laid the cards on the counter.

"Let's have a look see." He picked them up and looked through them, his eyes got wide. "Where did you come across these?"

Trey explained everything to him.

"I can't afford to give you anything close to what these are worth, but let me make a few phone calls."

"Thank you, my friend."

"Don't tell to many people about these. People will try and take advantage of you. These are worth a lot of money."

"I know, I did some checking last night."

"I'm glad you are saving the farm. I had heard rumors and felt bad for you."

"Thanks."

"Here let me give you something." He went behind the counter and came up with a small box.

"What's this?"

"These are plastic holders; they will keep the cards safe. These are in perfect condition and I would hate for something stupid to happen to them."

"What do I owe you?"

"A beer the next time we go out."

"Done."

They shook hands and Peter pulled him in for a hug.

"I am very happy for you." Peter said as he released the hug.

"Thank you. Hey how are the wife and kid doing?" Trey smiled.

"She left me two weeks ago, for some guy she works with."

"I'm sorry I didn't know."

"I haven't really been telling anyone. I have Ashley, she hasn't seen her in two weeks."

"Wow."

"My mom is helping me with her."

"We need to get together and catch up."

"That would be great. Give me a call."

"I will."

"I'll call you when I have more information for you."

"Great thanks."

Chapter Twenty

"What's wrong?" Clayton asked as he walked in.

Trey looked up from his phone and he was clearly stressed out.

"You know how expensive even used equipment is." He laid his phone on the table.

It had been a week and a half and Peter came through for him. He got top dollar for the cards, and it was enough to buy the farm, with very little left.

"Well at least you don't have a bank payment. You could mortgage the house." Clayton half smiled at him.

"I don't want to do that. What if I have a bad year, and then lose the farm again."

"What are you going to do then?"

"I'm not sure, there has to be another way."

"Have you talked to mom today, how is dad?"

"He is slowly getting better. Chris is going over a lot, that is lifting his spirits."

"That's great. I'm off to the shower." He headed upstairs and Trey went back to his phone.

A short time later Clayton came back down and Trey was still scrolling.

"Come up with anything?"

"We could turn part of the property into a camp ground." He smiled at him.

"If that's what you want to do."

"It's not." Trey laid his phone down again. "Why would anyone camp here."

"Maybe add a waterpark."

"I don't think so. That would be more expensive than the farm equipment."

"Probably."

"Who's here?" Trey said as a knock came at the door.

"Hi, can I help you?" Trey saw a tall beefy man with dirty blond hair and brown eyes standing at the door.

"Hey Trey. Do you know who bought your place?"

Trey looked confused for a minute, then realized it was Hunter. He was Stan's age and lived on the farm next door.

"Yeah me. Why?"

"We were going to buy it; we need the hay fields."

"Oh."

"Can we talk?"

"Sure, I guess." He followed Trey into the kitchen and sat down.

"So, I was wondering if you would be interested in selling off the two fields next to our property?"

"I don't think so. This farm has been in the family for four generations. I don't want to be the one to break it up."

"I understand. I feel the same way about our farm. Since my dad passed away two years ago, I've been running it. We are doing more corn this year so we have less fields for hay."

"Sorry about your loss."

"Thank you, sorry to hear about your dad as well."

"He is doing better."

"Good, as I was saying we need more hay, and I really don't want to have to buy it, that would eat a lot of the profits from the corn."

"I guess it probably would."

"You don't want to sell, you're sure?"

"I am."

"Then I have another offer."

"What is that?" Trey was already over this conversation.

"What if you lease the fields to me, say for a five- or ten-years period. You don't lose the land and you make some money."

Trey perked up now. "That might work."

"I know you sold everything already and need to rebuild. So, you probably won't be able to keep up with everything right away."

Trey just looked at him, not liking how much he knew about what was going on. Even though he knew rumors had been going around about the farm.

"You make some very good points."

"Thank you." He smiled at Trey.

"You know what, let me talk to my family, and my lawyer. I want to make sure we do this legal so no one gets hurt in the end."

"I am on board with that. I have already talked to my lawyer; he is the one who suggested the lease."

"Thank you for coming by. I will be in contact in the next couple of days." Trey stood and put his hand out.

"I look forward to doing business with you." He stood, shook Trey's hand and left.

"This is good and bad." Clayton said after he was gone.

"Now you want to talk." Trey gave him a dirty look.

"You do remember our dad and his dad did not get along at all?"

"I do. It all stemmed from an auction bidding war or something."

"Yes, on the other hand, this is a great idea and will help you out a lot."

"What do you think dad would say?"

"I think he would fight it, but in the end, he would see the value and do it."

"I think so to. I am going to call the lawyer, but first let's go see dad and tell him and mom."

They headed out the door. "You know that his mom and ours still sit together at church. They have been friends since grade school." Clayton said as they got in the car.

"I did not."

"They both think the fight is so silly, that neighbors should be friends."

"Well, then that's on our side."

Chapter Twenty-One

A few weeks later Trey was having dinner with Peter.

"My treat, you really hooked me up." Trey smiled as they looked at the menus.

"You don't have to do that."

"I want to, by the way where is Ashley tonight."

"My mom is babysitting. I was going to bring her but mom said I needed a night out."

"Well mom knows best."

"They think they do." They both laughed.

"Have you heard from your ex?"

"I know they moved out of state, I think Oklahoma."

"What really?"

"Yeah, he was from there and she wanted to find herself or something like that."

"That sucks."

"Thank God, Ashley has stopped asking for her mommy so much. Now when she is in trouble, she asks for grammy."

"Well, at least you have a support, that's great."

"So enough about me, tell me about this lease."

"Well, I signed it yesterday. We met in the middle on the price, but it's enough to keep me going with the rest of the farm."

"How long is the lease."

"Seven years, He wanted ten, I wanted five."

"Seems like a good deal."

"Yeah, I think I surprised him. He thought I was just going to do what he wanted."

"Was he happy in the end."

"For the most part I think."

Their food arrived and they ate in quiet.

"That was really good. Thank you." Peter said as he wiped his mouth and put the napkin on the table.

"I can't believe that's all you got, do you want some dessert or something?"

"No, no I'm good." Peter smiled at him a little differently than usual. It made Trey feel a little weird.

"Well, I have a lot to do tomorrow." Trey smiled as they both stood.

"Ok, I'll talk to you soon." Peter smiled again, then started to turn away. He stopped turned back and gave him a hug. "Thanks for the night out, I did need it."

"It was just dinner. It was my pleasure."

Peter left Trey standing there confused. Then he thought, he just needs a friend right now he is hurting. He paid the bill and left.

He got home and Chris and Anna were setting at the table smiling.

"What's going on here?"

"I have great news." Anna smiled big.

"What?"

"Your dad is coming home."

"What? How?"

"Well, he still needs a lot of help. We will have a nurse coming in daily, but Chris and I are going to do the majority of the care giving."

"This is great!"

"It's going to save a lot of money."

"But what about your job?"

"I'm taking an early retirement. I invested wisely several years ago and have a nice nest egg."

"This is great news."

"We have to make the living room a bed room for him, with a hospital bed for now." Anna continued.

"Whatever we need to do."

"How do you feel about Chris living here, only because if I need help and you're in the fields…"

"I don't have a problem with that."

"I'm still going to keep my place. As soon as I'm not needed, I'll move back home."

"I don't have a problem at all." Trey repeated and hugged him.

"Everything is ordered so within a week it will all be here. We just need to move the stuff out of the living room." Anna continued. "Oh, how did your date go?"

"It wasn't a date."

"Oh." Chris smiled.

"It was dinner with a friend. He is straight."

"Sorry." Anna smiled.

"And we had a nice time, dinner was good." He went upstairs before more questions came.

Chapter Twenty-Two

Trey woke the next morning, having had weird dreams about him and Peter. They were a couple at one point then Peter was yelling at him telling him he wasn't gay. He was so confused, he never thought about Peter that way.

"Stan you're here?" Trey was shocked to see him.

"Yeah, got someone to come build a ramp, he was able to be here first thing this morning. I wasn't sure what you were doing, so I came down."

"That's good. I am meeting with a guy in about an hour about a used tractor."

"Good, how is everything else going?"

"Good, the lease is done. This afternoon I'm going to see about buying two cows."

"I'm happy for you, you always loved the farm."

"Thanks." Trey went and got a cup of coffee and just looked out the kitchen window."

"What's wrong?"

Trey was quiet for a few moments, then looked at Stan.

"I'm confused."

"About?"

"Peter."

"Come again?" Stand was confused as well.

"My friend Peter, the pawn shop guy."

"Oh, OK."

Trey looked at him for a moment, then shook his head.

"I'm not confused about that at all you ass."

"Sorry, what has you confused. Isn't he married."

"She left him, and we had dinner last night."

"Oh, that's nice. A date?"

"No, I took him to dinner for helping me with the cards." He looked at Stan for a minute, then sighed.

"What?" Stan tried to play innocent.

"Mom already talked to you didn't she."

"I don't know what you mean?"

"That's why you're here." He shook his head.

Stan just smiled at him.

"Fine, it wasn't a date, but he gave me a look that made me feel uncomfortable. Then when he went to leave, he stopped turned and came back and hugged me, maybe held it a little too long."

"I see."

"That's all you have to say?"

"What do you want me to say?"

"I don't know, you're the older brother that mom sent to advise me or something I guess."

"OK, this is what I think. Peter is hurting right now; she left him for another guy and he is lonely. Maybe he has feelings for you, maybe not, he just needs company right now and it seems like feelings. Only time will tell."

"That is no help at all."

"Do you have feelings for him is the real question?"

Trey stood for a few moments. "I could."

"That's not a good answer. Don't try and feel something that's not there. It won't last and you will hurt your friendship."

"He is a good friend. I just never thought of him that way."

"Then take your time, just be friends. If it's meant to be then it will happen."

"How long did you talk to mom."

"Two hours last night."

"I knew this sounded more like her than you."

"Maybe, but I agree with it all. No need to rush anything."

"I guess so."

"I think my guy is here." Stan stood as a truck pulled in.

They walked outside and talked to the guy, and soon he was working on the ramp.

"Well, I'm going to see about that tractor, then head on over to buy the cows. I'll talk to you later." Trey smiled at Stan, who grabbed him and pulled him in for a hug.

"Don't stress, you have a family who loves and supports you. You can do anything." Stan said in his ear, then left him go.

"Thanks bro." Trey pulled his keys from his pocket and left.

He went and looked at the tractor, it was going to take more work than it was worth, so he passed on it. Disappointed he went to look at the cows.

He walked into the barn and started looking at the cows. They all looked really good, he smiled at least he was going to accomplished something today. He just had to find a way to get them home.

"Hey neighbor." Trey looked to see Hunter walking up to him.

"Hi, how are you?" Trey smiled, still not really sure how to feel about him.

"Just came to get some calves. I guess you're doing the same."

"Yeah, just two to start. It's going to take time to build back up."

"I guess."

"How are things going with you?"

"Well, it's just me and my brother and we can't handle everything. Trying to hire some help, but no one wants to work."

"I hear you."

"I had a guy last week behind the barn getting high on meth. Sent him packing, and he didn't understand why."

"Maybe I should just stay small." Trey half laughed.

"Do you know anyone who wants to work?"

"I don't, but if you need help from time to time, I may be able to help you. At least until I get things up and running again."

"Are you serious?" Hunter looked a little shocked.

"It would give me some extra money, that's always good." Trey couldn't believe what he was saying.

"I will keep you in mind."

The man came over and started to talk to Trey.

"Do you have a trailer I could rent from you to get them home?"

"I don't. The axle is broken on the trailer I rent out from the last guy that used it."

"OK, then. I'm going to wait till I can find a way to get them home." Trey shook his head, and walked away.

"Don't take too long first come first serve." The man said as he walked away.

"Did you get your two?" Hunter asked as he walked by.

"No, he doesn't have a trailer I can rent, so I have to find one first."

"Just wait a minute." Hunter said to him, and Trey stopped and looked at him.

A few minutes later Hunter was back.

"I have a deal for you."

"I feel like this is becoming a habit." Trey weakly smiled.

"I will buy you three calves and dropped them off for you, you work for me three to four days a week for the next month." Hunter smiled at him.

Trey just looked at him confused by the offer.

"How many hours a week?"

"Say thirty to thirty-five."

"Why would you do this?"

"First our fathers fight was stupid and I want to have a good relationship with you, second it solves both of our problems. That gives me time to find someone who wants to work, and you get your calves home, to start your rebuild."

"OK, fine done." They shook hands.

Chapter Twenty-Three

The next morning Trey came down grabbed a coffee and a bowl of cereal.

"So, it's true?" His mother asked as she sipped on her coffee.

"That depends on what you are referring to." Trey said as he wolfed another spoon of cereal down.

"You're working for Hunter?"

"Oh, well we made a deal that benefited both of us. So, I guess the short answer is yes."

"I see."

"What?"

"Nothing." She waved her hand in the air.

"Clearly it's something."

"Just don't get taken advantage of."

"I'm not mom. Right now, we are helping each other out. When it stops benefiting both of us..."

"Just be careful. I love his mother to death, but his father."

"His father passed away."

"I know, but he can be just like him. While being a good neighbor is good."

"Don't worry mom. I got this." He drank the milk from his bowl and put it in the sink. "I'll be careful." He kissed her on the head and headed out the door.

"Good morning." Hunter said as Trey got out of his truck.

"Good morning, what's the plan for today?"

"You're going to help my brother with the cows this morning. Got to get them milked. I should be back with a load of hay till you're done."

"Well, who is this stud?" A girl came out of the house.

"Oh, Valery, this is Trey. He is going to help us for about a month or so."

She walked up to him. Her brown hair hanging loosely over her shoulders. Her green eyes smiled at him in a way that made him feel like a piece of meat.

"This is my girlfriend, Trey."

"Nice to meet you." She walked behind him running her finger over his shoulders.

"Yeah, nice to meet you." Trey walked away from her.

"Don't worry about her she is harmless."

"OK." Trey said not sure about that.

"Valery go help mom." He shook his head. "Daren come on!" he yelled toward the house.

A young man came from the house. "Sorry, mom needs some help."

"No problem, Take Trey here and go milk the cows. I should be back with a load of hay by then."

Trey looked a Daren, who had black hair and brown eyes. He had the perfect five o'clock shadow and a smile that made him weak in the knees. He was just slightly smaller than Trey and almost as beefy. He had boots, tight jeans and a Star Wars t shirt. Trey liked everything he saw. He was happy to work with him.

"Come on Trey, let's get away from Valery." Daren motioned for him to follow him.

They walked down to the barn and moved the cows into their stalls and got the milking equipment going.

"Nice, you know what you're doing." Daren smiled at him.

"Yeah, you guys have better equipment than we do, or did. But it works the same." Trey smiled at him.

They made some more small talk, and Trey found himself nervous around him.

"So, what did you think of Valery?" He asked after a while.

"Well, she seems friendly." Trey smiled not wanting to be mean.

"That's a word for it. I call it being a slut." He laughed.

"I take it you don't like her?"

"Not even a little bit, and neither does my mom."

"I see, why does he date her then."

"He loves her, God knows why, and doesn't see a problem."

"You do?"

"She has tried to get with me several times. Everyone that comes here to work she hits on."

"Yeah, she made me a little uncomfortable."

"She does that a lot, that's why we can't keep workers."

"Wow, that sucks."

"Yeah, what about you, got a girlfriend."

Trey thought for a minute. "No, to busy trying to rebuild the farm for anything like that." He decided it would be better not to go into details.

"Yeah, I had a girlfriend, but she wanted me to go to college and get off the farm. I love this farm."

"I know what you mean."

"With all the work that needs done who has time for a personal life."

"I know man." Trey wished he would change the subject, because he just wanted to ask him out in the worst way. That would end badly he thought.

"Here comes Hunter, with the hay. Here give me that." He was right behind Trey now breathing on his neck. He could smell him, the soap from his shower this morning and the deodorant he had on. Old spice he thought. The combination wafted into his nose and made him forget where he was.

"Dude." Daren pushed him with his arm.

"What?" Trey came back. "I'm sorry here." He handed him the last suction tubes.

"Are you ok?"

"Yeah." He went to get up, and realized he had a tent. He went back down to his knees.

"What's wrong?" Daren looked at him weird.

"Leg went to sleep just give me a minute."

"Want a hand up?"

"No, no I'm fine."

Daren looked at him for a moment and then headed toward the hay wagon coming in. Once he was gone Trey stood and tried to adjust himself. He stayed down below and let the two of them go up in the loft to stack the hay.

"Ok, gents it's lunch." Hunter said as the two of them climbed out of the loft.

"I have something in my truck. See you guys in a few." Trey smiled.

"No way, mom made lunch come eat with us." Daren slapped him on the shoulder.

"That's ok." He could feel himself waking up from the slap.

"Mom won't have it any other way." Hunter smiled at him, now come on.

"Ok." Trey smiled.

"Daren said you did a great job this morning."

"Well, it's not like I'm new at this." Trey laughed.

"Hi you must be Trey." A lady about his mother's age met them at the door. "I was just about to yell for you boys."

"Trey this is my mother, Gale."

"It's very nice to meet you. Your mother talks about you boys all the time. I'm glad to have you here." She opened the door, and they all went in for lunch.

"Oh, Trey sit beside me." Valery pulled back a chair.

"You know that's Hunters chair." Gale scolded her, in a voice that let you know she didn't care for her.

"Trey, sit beside me." Daren pulled out a chair.

Trey looked and smiled weakly, then sat beside Daren, but right across from Valery.

"This is good, I get a nice view for lunch."

"Please, Valery, not at the table." Gale scolded her again.

"She is just playing mom." Hunter said as he sat down.

It was a wooden table they sat at, but not real big, Trey and Daren were shoulder to shoulder and feeling him so close was causing problems again.

"Ok, Let's pray." They held hands to pray. Trey ended up holding Daren and Valery's hands. Trey closed his eyes as the electricity from Daren was running through him, it was putting him over the edge. Then suddenly Daren let go of his hands and he opened his eyes. They started eating and Valery took her foot and put in Trey's crotch. Lunch was over and Trey was thankful that he was cleaning the barn by himself and Daren was helping his brother elsewhere.

Chapter Twenty-four

Then next morning Trey showed up. He wondered how he was going to survive a month.

"Good morning stud." Valery was waiting on the porch for him.

"Good morning. Where is Hunter?" Trey wasn't thrilled she was the first one he saw.

"They had to run to town quick this morning. You're supposed to start with the cows."

"OK, thanks." He turned and headed toward the barn.

"You know, I know."

Trey stopped not sure what she met. He turned slowly and looked at her.

"You held my hand and it gave you a hard on. I felt it with my foot."

"You did." He smiled a little. She has it so wrong he thought.

"It's OK, you play hard to get. I like a challenge."

"OK, then." He turned to go again.

"You are well hung I can tell." She called after him.

He just kept walking to the barn. He went about taking care of the cows and muttering to himself about how did he end up in this situation.

"You always talk to yourself?"

He looked back to see Daren standing there.

"Oh hey, well, only when I'm frustrated."

"What's going on?"

"Just personal stuff." Trey decided he didn't know how to tell him the truth.

He came up beside Trey and started helping him clean the last of the suction tubes. He could smell him again, and it was driving him crazy.

"It's almost lunch." Daren finally said.

"Yeah, it is." Trey dreaded the idea of having to deal with Valery again.

"Don't worry you can sit beside me again." He laughed.

"Actually, I have to go take care of a few things quick. I'll be back after lunch."

"Mom's not going to be happy about that."

"Please tell her I am sorry." Trey loved the idea of sitting next to him again, but not dealing with her.

Trey grabbed his phone and made a call as soon as he was out of site.

"Hey, what are you doing?... Good can we meet for lunch? Really you need to talk to me as well. Great, let's just meet as Sheetz. Ok. see you there."

Trey sat there waiting. He just got a coffee his nerves were too far gone to be able to eat.

"Hey there you are." Benton sat down at the table across from him.

"Things are a little crazy for me right now. I'm not sure what I should do."

"You mean with Peter?"

"No. Wait, how do you know about that?"

"I stopped in this morning and your mom told me."

"Figures."

"What's going on?"

"I'm working for the neighbor and his girlfriend is all over me, and on top of that I am attracted to his younger brother."

"Yikes."

"When you say all over you."

"At lunch yesterday she put her foot in my crotch."

"Shit!"

"It gets worse. I had a hard on because I was setting right next to the brother, who smell is making me very horny, and she thinks she is the reason."

Benton tried to hold in his chuckle but failed.

"It's not funny."

"Is the brother gay?"

"He is straight."

"Wow. That's an ugly situation."

"The brother and the mother know she is a slut, but he loves her." Trey was still shaking his head.

"I'm sorry dude."

"What did you have to talk to me about?"

"Maybe another time." Benton started to get up.

"Oh, come on. It's fine, tell me."

"Well, I know I told you that I wasn't ready to date yet and all."

"OK." Trey got a smile on his face.

"I'm have been on a couple of dates with someone we both know."

"Ok" Trey's smile faded.

"It's Shane."

"From school."

"Yes."

"Wait I thought he moved out west."

"His company down sized so he moved back here."

"And he is gay?"

"Has been for a long time. He just didn't want me to tell anyone."

"What?" Trey looked confused.

"We messed around after we were out of school. We both like the same things, I'm very attracted to him."

"But not me."

"Not in the same way. He wanted to come to, but I wanted to talk to you first."

"You don't even want to give us a chance?"

"It would never work, and our friendship would be hurt."

"He makes you happy?"

"Yes, I think he will."

"Then I guess I'm happy for you."

"You have two guys and a girl to deal with right now anyway. There is no room for me." Benton tried to joke.

"I really don't know what to do." He looked at his phone. "Crap I got to get back."

"Listen are we ok?"

"Yes, you're my best friend. I can't say that I'm not disappointed, and you will always have a piece of my heart."

"Shane wants us to get together and have coffee."

"Maybe, I have a lot on my plate right now."

"Call me."

"I will, you're not getting rid of me just yet."

They hugged, but it didn't feel the same as it used to for Trey. He raced back to the farm.

"Sorry, man my meeting ran a little long."

"It's fine, just go help Daren in the barn. I have to go check the fields, there is a problem with the watering system."

"Always something." Trey smiled.

He went to the barn and helped Daren put the supplies away and clean the barn. His smell was still driving him crazy. They made small talk, but Trey had a hard time concentrating. He just kept thinking what it would be like to be with him.

Chapter Twenty-five

Trey sat at the kitchen table thankful he wasn't working over at the neighbors today. His brother has given him two dozen chickens and he needed to do some repairs to the fence around the coupe. He was home alone and he was thankful for the peace and quiet. He finished his breakfast and headed out the door.

"Well, not working today?"

Trey couldn't believe his eyes. Valery was standing beside her car waiting for him.

"Why are you here?" Trey just looked annoyed at her

"I've done a little research on you." She smiled and started walking toward him.

"Have you now?" He was a little nervous, hoping she didn't do too much research.

"Yes, turns out, you are as big of a tramp as I am."

"Is that what you thing?"

"From the list of girls, I know you have dated, maybe bigger."

"I doubt that."

"You see, most girls would be offended by that, but not me."

"Won't they wonder where you are?" Trey was over the conversation and headed to the chicken house.

"I said I was going shopping. They won't expect me back for a while."

"What happens when you show up with nothing."

"You know I love the chase." She chose to ignore his last question.

"Good for you."

"We got time you know, you're alone…"

"I don't think so."

"And why not?" She ran and jumped in front of him.

"Are you serious. You are the girlfriend of a man I am doing business with on several levels."

"He doesn't care."

"I do." He pushed her out of the way.

"You have a girlfriend don't you."

"Nope, single and like it that way."

"That's what's great, I don't want a relationship, just a smash and go."

"Do you hear yourself?"

"I do." She smiled.

"Well, you're barking up the wrong tree." He started walking again.

"I will have you. You will give in."

"Nope." He just kept walking.

She stopped her feet and walked back to her car and pealed out of the drive way.

By lunch he had the fence fixed and had taken care of the few animals he had. He walked back into the house and fixed himself a sandwich. He went to eat and his phone went off.

"Peter, buddy, what's up?" Trey answered.

"Hey I'm having a cook out tonight, want to come over?"

"Sure, need me to bring anything?"

"Nope."

"What time?"

"Eating around five thirty or so."

"See you then."

He finished his sandwich and headed to his appointment; he was looking at another tractor. It was around four when he pulled up to Peter's house.

"I'm glad you could make it. I invited a couple of other friends over." Peter said as he opened the door.

"Thanks, oh my God is that little Ashley." Trey said as he reached for her. She looked at him and ran the other way laughing.

"Even she thinks you're funny looking." Peter smiled at him.

"Got the jokes. Good to see you smiling."

It was almost six and no one else had shown up.

"Well, we might as well eat." Peter sighed.

"Hot dog daddy." Ashley jumped up and down as he put them on the grill.

"Yes, baby. Just a minute." He put a couple of burgers on as well.

Soon the food was ready and they were sitting at the picnic table fixing their plates.

"Where is the barbeque sauce?" Trey looked around.

"Oh, it's over by the grill, I'll get it." Peter got up, grabbed it turned to come back to the table and tripped over his own feet. The bottle went flying toward Trey who tried to catch it, but as he grabbed it the lib popped off and sauce went all over him.

"Oh my god I'm so sorry." Peter grabbed some paper towels to help clean him up. Ashley sat eating her hot dog and laughing.

"It's OK." He grabbed some of the paper towels and they both tried to clean him up, as they laughed.

"Well, it's almost all cleaned up." Peter said as he grabbed another paper towel, he took it and started to gently wipe his face. He put the paper towel down, and they locked eyes.

"Um, thank you." Trey finally said.

"You still have a little sauce here." Peter took his thumb and wiped it off the side of his chin. Just as he started to pull his hand away Trey grabbed it and sucked the sauce off his thumb. They looked each other in the eyes again they both started to lean in for a kiss.

"Sorry, we are late." Came voices as the door opened.

"It's OK. We are out here making a mess." Peter laughed.

"I'm going to go clean up more." Trey smiled and walked into the house.

He rejoined the party a short time later, and everything had been cleaned up.

"Are you hungry yet?" Peter smiled, but Trey could feel the weirdness between them now.

"No, I feel very sticky yet. I think I am going to go home and get a shower."

"You can take one here if you want."

"No, that's OK."

"OK, well don't be a stranger." Peter half smiled again.

"I won't." Trey smiled and left.

Chapter Twenty-six

"I am so stupid." Trey complained to himself as he pulled into Sheetz to get gas. "He is never going to talk to me again." Trey slammed his door, and put his card in the gas pump.

"Trey!" He heard a voice from across the parking lot. He looked and Shawn was coming across the parking lot.

"Shane." Trey almost groaned. "Not now." Trey said to himself.

"How are you buddy?"

"I've been better." He smiled for the half.

"Do I smell barbecue sauce?"

"Yes. Don't ask long story." Trey took a deep breath.

"Listen I hope you not mad at me."

"What?" Trey's mind was a million miles away.

"About Benton."

"Oh, no. He made it clear a while back that we were just friends."

"Is something wrong?"

"What do you mean?"

"You seem very distracted."

Trey sighed heavy and he finished pumping his gas and put the cap back on.

"I may have just fucked up a good friendship. I feel like I am going crazy."

"Want to talk I am a good listener?"

"Talk? With you?" Trey just stared at him.

"I have changed since high school, it's not all about me anymore."

"I really got to go home and shower."

"The barbeque sauce?"
"Yes."
"I could come by for coffee."
"Really?"
"Why not. We got catching up to do anyway."
"What about Benton?"
"First we have only been on two dates, and second it's just coffee."
Trey thought for a few minutes. "Ok, fine see you at the house."
"OK." Shane smiled and walked back to his car.

A short time later Trey was coming down the stairs after taking his shower, and Shawn was waiting with a fresh pot of coffee ready.

"So, what happen?"
"What happen to catching up?"
"We will."
"I was at a friend's house and we almost kissed, but his friends showed up and interrupted it."
"So, why is that bad?"
"He was all weird after that."
"What about you?"
"What about me?"
"Do you like him?"
"Not in that way. Does that make me sound bad."
"Then why were you going to kiss him."
"I was just in the moment. He was wiping sauce off my face; I sucked the sauce off his thumb."
"You what? You left that out."
"It all seemed a blur. I have been so worked up lately I feel like I'm going to explode."
"Worked up about what?"
"There is this other guy, that I have been working with. He is very good looking and his smell makes me very horny."
"Oh, so you were thinking about him when you almost kissed this other guy."

Trey just looked at him, and Shane knew the answer was yes without him answering.

"So asked this other guy out."

"He is straight."

"Does he know you're gay?"

"No. I didn't say anything, I didn't want problems there. I have deals with that family now."

"OK."

"There is a lot riding on this and I don't want to mess it up."

"I wasn't judging."

"Enough about me. Tell me about you."

"Well, it took me some time to come to terms with who I am, but I'm ok with it now."

"Your family?"

"For the most part. Some extended family won't talk to me, but that's their loss not mine."

"Good way to look at it."

"When I was out west, I met a guy who help me a lot. He showed me how to be a dominate caring top, not just an ass like I was in school."

"Did you know when you were in school?"

"Yes, but never said anything."

"Me to. Benton told me once he really enjoyed how we treated him in the locker room that day."

"He does love it rough."

"I know." Trey seemed a little sad.

"I do love him you know."

"I hope so."

"We are just dating. He still isn't ready for a serious relationship."

"I am, but I can't find anyone."

"You have two guys right now, what are you talking about?"

"You're funny."

"You will find that person. You're a sweet guy."

"They say nice guys finish last."

"What do they know?" Shane waved his hands in the air.

"I have to go check on my animals."

"Yeah, I should get going, work in the morning." He stood to leave.

"Thank you." Trey stood and smiled at him.

"I'm glad we are friends."

"We have always been and always will be."

Shane walked over to him and grabbed him, hugging him tight. Trey returned the hug.

"You know some of the other guys, from school, know and have shied away from me. I think their loss, but it still bothers me."

"I really don't talk to anyone from school anymore." Trey shrugged his shoulders.

"That's probably for the best." Shane looked at him again, and pulled him in for another hug.

"I'll call you. You me and Benton should hang out." Shane looked like he might cry.

"That would be cool." Trey said not sure if he was going to be able to handle that.

He followed Shane to his car and waved good bye as he pulled out. Then went to check on his animals. He had to go to work at the neighbors in the morning and he wasn't looking forward to it.

Chapter Twenty-Seven

"Good morning." Valery smiled at Trey as he got out of his truck.

"Good morning. Where are the guys?" He didn't like the idea of being alone with her.

"They will be back later. You are supposed to do the cows." She walked toward him.

"Just stop right there." Trey put his hand up.

"Still trying to stop the inevitable? Just let it happen and enjoy it."

"What does Hunter say about this behavior?"

"He doesn't understand me. I bet you would."

"I don't think so."

"Valery, leave him alone!" Gale yelled from the porch.

"She always spoils everything." She sighed and turned and went back into the house.

"Good morning." Trey waved at Gale.

"Good morning, dear. I'll see you at lunch."

"OK." Trey smiled and made his way to the barn.

Time went slow and the cows didn't want to cooperate.

"Not cooperating again today I see." Daren said as Trey cursed at another cow.

"Not even a little today." Trey grumbled.

"Mom said Valery was after you again."

"She was." Trey rolled his eyes.

"Listen after lunch we are going to clean the top of the barn."

"I told Hunter I could only work till noon today. They are delivering my dad's bed and he is coming home later this afternoon."

"That's great."

Trey went to get up and slipped, Daren grabbed his arm to break his fall. Trey looked up and the smell of Daren overtook him and he couldn't talk.

"Are you OK?"

"Yeah." Was all he could manage.

"Well mom has lunch ready; I'll help you finish up quick."

"Yeah, thanks." Trey finally got out. He was glad he wasn't working with him this afternoon.

He sat beside Daren at lunch and Valery tried to flirt with him again, and he just ignored her. He was lost in Daren smell.

He got home just as the guys with the bed got there.

"Perfect timing." Trey smiled at them.

"Where is it going?" The man smiled at him.

"Follow me." He took them into the living room. All the furniture had been moved out two days ago.

"OK, let me get this set up and I'll show you how to use it."

A short time later he was done and showed Trey how to use the remote.

"Seems easy enough."

"OK, here is the paper work, if you need anything call this number." He pointed to a number on the paper.

He left and Trey made a pot of coffee and waited for his dad to come home. He had gone to see him several times at the nursing home, but he was looking forward to seeing him every day again. A car pulled up and he jumped and ran to the door.

"Clayton, where is dad?" Trey looked confused.

"Come with me, we are going to the hospital."

"Why?" Trey slammed the door shut and ran to the car.

"Dad started running a fever this morning."

"Why? From what?"

"They aren't sure. They took him to the hospital; they were admitting him when I left."

They got to the hospital and Stan and Eddie were standing outside.

"What's going on?" Trey asked as they got to them.

"He has a staff infection." Stan told them.

"Is he going to be, OK?" Clayton asked.

"They are going to keep him for a couple of days. They started antibiotics. You two go in, we talked to him already. Room 412."

They headed in and soon found his room.

"You two boys visit with your dad. I'm going for some coffee." Anna smiled at them. She looked like she had aged twenty years in the last month. They had all tried to get her to get some rest, but she was having none of it.

Trey looked at his dad all hooked up to tubes again. He had seen this several times since he has been in and out of the hospital, but it never got easier. A nurse came in and put some medicine in his IV.

"He is resting, the infection has made him very tired." She smiled at them, then put some information in the computer, and left.

They sat there looking at each other saying nothing lost in their own thoughts.

Chapter Twenty-Eight

Trey got home late; his dad slept the whole time he was there. He poured a cup of cold coffee and threw it in the microwave.

"Hey Trey you home?" Came a voice from the front door. He looked and Daren was standing there.

"Hey, did you need something?" Trey walked to the door trying to hold back how happy he was to see him.

"I saw you coming down the road. I just wanted to check on you."

"Come in I'll start a pot of coffee."

"No need to do that. I'm not staying long, and you look tired."

"Well, dad is in the hospital, with an infection. I was there most of the day. He just slept."

"I stopped by earlier and no one was here. I figured something must have happened."

They both moved to sit on the steps.

"It's hard to see him that way." Trey just hung his head.

"I know, it was hard to see my dad that way."

"I want to go see him tomorrow. I won't be at work."

"I understand. Hunter will be fine with it."

"I'm tired, but I don't think I will sleep well."

"Did you eat at all?"

"No."

"Do you want to go grab a bite to eat?"

"No, I'm too tired."

"OK, I'm going to go then. If you need anything just call."

"Thanks, you're so kind."

They stood and looked at each other for a minute. Daren grabbed him and pulled him in for a hug.

"I'm sorry about your dad."

"Thank you." Trey hugged him back. Smelling him made him feel calm and safe. He didn't want to let go.

"I was very close to my dad to. I wish I could have one more day with him." He whispered in his ear. His warm breath on his ear and neck, almost made him moan out loud.

"I will talk to you tomorrow?" Trey smiled as they stopped hugging.

"Take care of your dad. I'll see you when you come back to work." He smiled and walked to his car.

Trey watched him leave wishing he was staying the night with him. It would have been nice to have him to snuggle with.

He walked back into the house, he put his cup in the sink and headed to bed. He laid in bed staring at the ceiling. He got up and got on his knees and bowed his head.

"God, I don't know if you're listening, but please take care of my father. I miss him so much. He is not happy now, I know that. He needs to be moving and doing things. Please help him to relax and give him the strength to get better. I pray in your name, amen."

He got up and got back into bed, and soon sleep took over. It had been a long day.

"Trey, listen son."

Trey opened his eyes and his dad was standing there. Then he looked around and he was standing in the barn. He was so confused.

"This is where you and me are the happiest. I love all the time we spent together."

"What's going on?"

"I wanted to tell you I love you. I know parents aren't supposed to have favorites, but between us. You're my favorite." His dad smiled at him.

"I miss working with you." Trey smiled.

"I want you to know I love you and I am proud of you, and the man you have become."

"Why are you telling me this?"

"My heart. The infection did more damage to it." His dad stopped and looked at him.

"Are you gone?" Trey knew without asking.

"I'm on my way. My parents and grandparents are waiting for me."

"I'm going to miss you so much."

"I'm going now, I have to talk to your mother, and time is short."

"I will continue to make you proud."

"I have no doubt."

Darkness came and Trey opened his eyes again as his phone was going off. It was his brother Stan. He knew what he was going to tell him and he didn't want to answer the phone.

Chapter Twenty-Nine

Trey got dressed and headed to the hospital after hanging up with his brother. It was three in the morning, and he still was not awake. Clayton had been at the hospital with their mother, Eddie, Stan his wife, and Chris were on their way there.

"Trey." His mother hugged him tightly when he walked into the room.

"Mom, I love you." Trey hugged her back and the tears he had been fighting broke lose.

"He called me to his side, held my hand." She couldn't say anymore.

"It's ok mom." Clayton joined Trey in hugging their mother.

Soon the rest of the family was there, all hugging each other and saying good bye to a man who had meant so much to all of them.

"Let's go back to the farm." Trey said

"I'll take mom." Clayton said.

They all left and headed back to the farm, soon they were sitting at the kitchen table. Stan was making coffee.

"I don't know what to do now." Anna looked at everyone.

"You and dad have a lot of things already in place." Stan reminded her.

"We are all here to do what needs done." Eddie added.

"We will make calls later today. For now, don't worry mom." Trey took her hand.

"I'm going to miss him so much." Anna squeezed Trey's hand.

"We all are." Eddie sighed.

The morning came, and word spread. Calls came as did friends with food and hugs. The undertaker said he would take care of things, that dad had everything paid for.

"Uncle Chris how are you doing?" Trey found him down by the barn.

"I'm hurting, just like the rest of the family." He turned and looked at Trey.

"I will miss him so much."

"I lost so much time, over what?" Chris sighed wiping tears now.

"You were here at the end. He was so happy to see you."

"I was happy to see him as well. Life is so short."

"Well, you are part of this family don't think about going anywhere." Trey grabbed him and hugged him.

They walked and talked about memories they had.

"There you are." Ruth said as they got back to the house.

"Yeah, sorry we just needed to take a break."

"Well, Alice is here with Carl and James. Benton and a friend are on their way."

"I figured." Trey nodded.

"And Peter is here."

"Oh." Trey was shocked.

"Who is he?" Chris looked at him.

"A friend."

Chris raised an eyebrow.

"No, he is straight."

"Trey, I'm so sorry." Peter came out of the house.

"Thanks, Peter." Trey half smiled still a little embarrassed from the picnic.

"Can we talk?" Peter whispered in his ear as he hugged him.

"Yeah, let's go for a walk."

They walked toward the barn.

"Listen I'm sorry about the other day." Trey started.

"There is nothing to be sorry about."

Trey looked over at him questioningly.

"I'm not saying I'm gay or even bi. I'm just not upset by what almost happen."

"You're not?"

"No, not at all. I'm touched really."

"I'm glad."

They were by the barn and Peter stopped and looked at him. The looks he gave him made him feel a little uncomfortable.

"Are you OK?" Trey finally asked.

Peter grabbed his face with both hands and kissed him so gently. Trey reached up and touched Peter's face gently as he pulled away. Peter said nothing turned, went to his car and left. Trey still in a daze walked back to the house as a car and truck were pulling in.

"Trey I'm so sorry for your loss." Hunter said as he and Daren got out of the truck.

"Me too." Daren chimed in.

"Mom and Valery are going to stay and help. We have to go back and finish some work." Hunter explained.

Trey looked over at the car as Gale and Valery were carrying covered dishes into the house.

"We have so much food. You guys should come back for dinner." Trey offered.

"Why do people always bring a ton of food at times like this?" Hunter shrugged.

"I'll come back." Daren smiled at him.

"Yeah, we will see you later. We just wanted to stop by and say how sorry we are, and come back to work when you're ready. We will work something out with the deal then." Hunter gave him a hug, followed by Daren.

Trey turned and walked toward the house. Chris was just coming out.

"There are so many people here." He smiled at Trey.

"What?" Trey could tell he wanted to asked a question.

"So."

"I don't really know."

"Well, that's OK. Take your time."

"I don't have the energy to deal with anything right now."

"That's too bad, there are several people in the house looking for you."

He put his arm around him and they walked into the house together.

Later that night after everyone left, he couldn't sleep and he came down to the kitchen.

"Couldn't sleep either?" Anna asked as she sipped on some coffee.

"No." He, said as he grabbed a glass of milk.

"He came to me." Trey said after a few minutes of silence.

"Did he?"

"I was asleep, and suddenly I was in the barn with him."

"That sounds about right."

"Told me he loved me and was proud of me."

"He needed you to know that. He knew coming out was hard for you, and that you worried about your relationship with him."

"He said his time was short and he had to get back to you."

"He made it back, long enough to say I'm sorry and I love you." She started to cry now.

"I'm sorry mom. I didn't mean to make you cry."

"You didn't. There are going to be a lot of tears in the next couple of days."

"I know."

"I know we should be happy for him. He is in a much better place, and he isn't suffering anymore."

"I know he couldn't have been happy at the end."

"He wasn't I know. Stuck in bed like that."

"Well, he is happy now."

"Till I get there." His mother giggled a little.

"That won't be for a long time yet." He leaned over and hugged her.

"We have a long couple of days, we should get some sleep."

"You're right." He put his glass in the sink, and headed up the stairs.
"Good night." She watched him go.
"You going to bed?"
"Soon." She smiled.

Chapter Thirty

The next couple of days seemed like a blur. Stan had taken Anna back to his place after the burial, she didn't think she could go back to the farm house yet. Trey found himself just standing looking at his dad's grave. It was covered in fresh dirt and the flowers on top still fresh.

"It doesn't get easier." Daren's voice came from behind him.

"What are you doing here?" Trey looked at him.

"Visiting my dad." Daren moved to stand beside Trey.

"I just can't believe he is gone."

"I spent several days down here after my dad past."

"I know I need to move on, but I feel like I'm forgetting him." Trey looked at him for reassurance.

"You're not, but I understand the feeling."

"I'll be at work in the morning."

"I'm glad, could use the help with the cows." He elbowed him.

"I'm glad I started working over there. I really enjoy our friendship." Trey said knowing he really wanted more.

"Well, we both have the same dislike for Valery. That was a good starting point."

Trey hung his head smiling for the first time in days. He sighed, turning and headed to his car.

"I'll see you in the morning then." Daren waved at him.

"Yes." Trey yelled back.

That night he didn't sleep well. He was home alone and it was very quiet, to quiet. Morning came fast and he was still tired.

"Well, well. There he is." Valery said as he got out of the truck.

"Doesn't mom need your help with something." Daren said as he walked up.

"Don't be jealous. You know I want you to." She turned and walked back into the house.

"Lucky us." Daren smiled at him.

"She is quite the slut."

"Never mind her."

They went about their day. Lunch was the same old thing with Valery, but Trey had gotten use to ignoring her.

"Well, I'll see you tomorrow." Trey said as he headed to his truck.

"Are you doing, OK?" Daren asked as he was about to shut the door.

"What do you mean?"

"Well, you said no one was home right now, being alone can't be easy right now."

Trey's mind raced with possibilities, none of which he thought would come true.

"I'm fine."

"OK, well mom said if you want to come over for dinner, you're welcome anytime."

"Thanks. I'm going to see a friend tonight, but maybe another time."

"Invites always open."

"Thanks."

Trey left and went home.

"Hey Peter, yeah I'm ready, OK see you there."

Trey headed out the door. Peter had called him that morning and wanted to meet and have a bite to eat. They met at a local diner, they both ordered burgers and fries.

"So, I wanted to say sorry." Peter started.

"Sorry, for what?" Trey looked confused.

"I shouldn't have kissed you like that, I'm not gay."

"It was fine."

"I don't know what came over me." Peter shook his head.

"It's OK."

"I looked at you and went right back to that night, and I just wanted the kiss."

"Why?" Trey thought let's see where this goes.

"I really don't know."

"Did you enjoy it?"

Peter just looked at him, smiled and lowered his head.

"That's ok, it was nice. I enjoyed it as well." Trey assured him.

"Yes, well I hope it doesn't affect our friendship."

"No, not at all."

Peter got silent and finished his burger. Trey just looked at him, knowing there was more to come.

"So, what's on your mind?"

"What? Nothing."

Trey just looked at him.

"It bothers me that I liked it."

"Ah, so you think you might be gay."

"No, I'm not, I have a daughter."

"And China has tea what's your point?"

"I don't know. I'm confused I guess."

"I see."

"What does that mean?"

"Nothing."

"I think I need to go home." Peter stood.

"OK. I'll pay." Trey pulled out his card.

Peter just looked at him, and walked out. Trey paid and walked to his car, and Peter was standing there.

"I don't know what to do?" Peter sighed.

"What do you mean?"

"You know what I mean."

Trey walked up to him, stood nose to nose, and whispered. "Are you saying you want more?"

"I don't know what I'm saying." Peter wanted to move but didn't

Trey grabbed him by the back of the neck, and pulled his face in and kissed him. Peter didn't fight it, and Trey held it for what seemed hours, but in seconds he left him go, walked him backwards, turned and got into his car and left.

Chapter Thirty-One

Trey drove home, he felt guilty kissing Peter like that. He knew he was straight just confused right now because of everything going on. He sat at his table having some cookies and milk before going to bed.

"This is nothing like mom's homemade." He looked at the cookie he had taken out of the store-bought package of cookies.

There was a knock at the door. Trey looked at his phone.

"Wonder who is here now." Trey muttered at he walked to the door.

"Hey." Peter smiled at him.

"What are you doing?"

"Can I come in?"

"Sure."

Peter followed Trey into the kitchen.

"What some cookies and milk?" Trey offered.

"Sure." Peter sat down, and Trey got him some milk.

"So, what do I owe this visit?"

"I think you know."

"Listen, I'm sorry. I know you're hurting right now. I shouldn't have done that to you."

"I am ok." Peter smiled at him.

They sat and ate their cookies for a few minutes.

"Where is Ashley?" Trey asked.

"She is spending the night with mom."

"I see."

"So, I thought." Peter stopped and just looked at Trey.

"Thought what?"

"Nothing." Peter shoved another cookie in his mouth.

"No, what?"

"I would like to spend some time with you." Peter smiled and turned beat red.

"Spend time?" Trey said with a mouth full of cookie.

"Are you going to make me spell it out."

Trey smiled.

"You know what maybe this was a bad idea." Peter went to get up.

"No, no. it's fine, but why?"

"I don't know. I enjoyed both kisses. Maybe I like guys, maybe not. It would explain my problems with girls."

"You have a problem."

"I never stay interested."

"Really?"

"I felt more aroused by you than I ever have with any girl."

"Are you sure?"

"I think I need to find out."

"OK, then."

They finished their milk and put their glasses in the sink. Trey looked up the stairs then back at Peter.

"Are you sure? I don't want to hurt our friendship."

"I'm sure."

Trey took his hand and they headed upstairs. Trey started undressing and Peter just stood there.

"Are you going to get undressed?"

"I'm a little nervous."

"We don't have to do anything. You don't have to stay."

"No, I'm fine." He started to get undressed.

They both undress and crawled into bed.

"So, what is it you want to do?"

"I don't know. I'm so nervous I think I might be sick."

"How about we just cuddle, and see what happens."

"OK." Peter smiled and rolled on his side.

Trey snuggled up close behind him and started kissing him on the back of the neck.

Trey took the hand under Peter's neck and held the bottom of his chin firmly as he ran his other hand over his chest. Peter started breathing hard and soon moved the hand from his chest slowly down to his crotch. Trey made him groan a little more then grabbed his arm and spun him around so they were face to face. He kissed him hard, then grabbed the back of his head and pushed him down.

A short time later they both lay on their back exhausted and smiled.

"Thank you." Peter smiled at him as he rolled over resting his head on his chest and his arm over his belly.

"Thank you I needed that to." Trey smiled and put his arm around him and they both fell asleep.

"Listen I have to get to work." Trey said the next morning as he was finishing his coffee, and Peter was just coming down the steps.

"OK I need to go myself."

"Are you OK?" Trey smiled at him.

"I am. I think."

"Good." Trey smiled and was heading toward the door.

"So." Peter started, and Trey stopped and looked back.

"So, what?"

"What are we now? This is a little confusing to me."

"I'm not looking for a relationship." Trey said.

"Me either. I was thinking friends with benefits."

"I'm OK with that."

"You know, because I don't want Ashley to know. I need to find her a mom." Peter sighed.

Trey wasn't sure how to take that, but just smiled at him.

"OK, I'll see you later. Lock the door on your way out."

Chapter Thiry-Two

Peter's words ran through Trey's head all day. It bothered him more that he thought it should. After all he wasn't really into Peter that way. It was nice being with him, but he didn't think he loved him like that.

"Dude you are a million miles away today what's wrong?" Daren asked as they finished some barn work.

"Nothing, just lots on my mind."

"We should go out for a drink tonight. Relax. You have had a lot going on lately."

"I don't think so. I have too much to do."

"Rain check, then."

"Don't you have other friends who would be more fun than me?"

"Please I'm a lot like you. Work on the farm all day. My friends from school have moved on or moved away. So, all I have is my brother, and he is all tied up with that slut."

"OK, then a rain check."

"And mom still wants to know when you are going to come over for dinner. She knows your mom is still with your brother."

"I'll come over tonight." Trey smiled. He didn't really want to deal with Valery, but a home cooked meal sounded good.

"Good mom will get off my back." Daren slapped him on the back.

"I'm going to go home and take care of things there. I'll be back. Just message what time to be here."

"No problem."

Trey came back later that night and had dinner. Valery smiled when she saw him.

"Did you miss me?" She smiled at him, while she ran her finger down his arm.

"No." He brushed her arm away from him.

"Dinner was great. Thank you." Trey said rubbing his belly.

"You're welcome my dear, anytime. I told your mother I would look after you till, she came home." She smiled at him.

"Hey you want to go for a ride on the quads." Daren offered.

"Sure." Trey agreed as he noticed Valery getting up.

"They went to the barn and jumped on the quads.

Trey followed Daren out trails through mud pits. They made it to a clearing and Daren stopped.

"Is something wrong?" Trey asked as he pulled up.

"Nope just got to piss." Daren said as he stepped into the wood line.

"Oh." Trey did his best to not look.

Daren finished and walked back to his quad and sat.

"I have a favor I want to ask you." Daren said not really looking at Trey.

"What is it?" Trey asked knowing it wasn't going to be what he was hoping.

"I know you said you're busy and all, and I know we are not like best friends."

"Just ask already."

"I have been talking to this girl on line and she said we could go on a date if I had a friend for her friend."

Trey just looked at him for a moment not sure if he was kidding or not.

"You don't have to." Daren finally said.

"No, no. I'll go I haven't been on a date in a long time. A double date sounds fun."

"Really?"

"Sure, why not." Trey couldn't believe what he was agreeing to.

"Great I'll set it up and let you know."

"Cool." Trey smiled the biggest fake smile ever.

"Race you back." Daren jumped on his quad and took off.

Trey took off, knowing he wasn't going to catch him.

"You are so slow." Daren laughed as Trey pulled in behind him.

"You cheated."

"Do you want to come in for coffee?"

"No, I should get home."

"You sure?"

"Yeah, got to figure out what to wear on the date."

"Aww, you two going on a date?" Valery came out of nowhere.

"I really hate when you eavesdrop like that." Daren groaned.

"Aw, sorry." She smiled at him. "So, when is this big date?"

"It's a double date if you must know." Trey snapped at her.

"Aww isn't that cute."

"You two could just have me and not have to go on a date."

"But we don't have time to go to the doctors the next day to get the medicine for whatever you give us." Daren snapped at her.

"I'm going home now." Trey smiled as he walked out.

"That was rude even for you." Valery yelled at him as Trey walked away.

Chapter Thirty-Three

Trey sat at the table the next morning drinking coffee and trying to figure out how he ended up on a double date.

"Hey bro." Clayton came strolling in.

"Hi." Trey casually waved at him.

"What's wrong?"

"I got myself into trouble." Trey sighed.

"Then he will marry you." Clayton tried to sound stern.

Trey rolled his eyes. "You're an idiot."

"So, what's wrong?"

"I may have agreed to go on a double date with a guy who I like."

"Wait, you're going on a date with him?"

"No, he is talking to a girl and she has a friend and she asked if he had a friend?"

"But you're gay."

"I know that, but he doesn't."

"And you said yes to this date."

"I did."

"Well, that should be a good time." Clayton laughed.

"Not funny."

"Just go have a good time. You don't have to sleep with this girl."

"True."

"Just bring her home to me, let her have a real man."

"Oh, God you are full of it today."

"Yeah, I have the next three days off, that always puts me in a good mood."

Trey looked at him and smiled as his phone went off.

"Hello."

"Hey I talked to the girls. You good for tonight at seven."

"Yeah, I guess that sounds good."

"Cool. I'll pick you up we are meeting them at Texas Roadhouse."

"I'll be ready." Trey hung up the phone and hung his head.

"So, what time is the big date?"

"Seven tonight."

"Good for you."

"Shut up."

A couple hours later Trey was sitting on the porch as Daren pulled up to pick him up.

"Thanks for doing this, man." Daren said as he got into the truck.

"So, what's wrong with her?" Trey said not really caring either way.

"Nothing."

"You know you owe me big."

"We will have fun relax."

They headed to Texas road house.

"So why are they meeting us there?"

"They didn't feel safe not knowing us that well."

"Really?"

"Well, more you than me." Daren smiled at him.

They got to the restaurant and the girls were waiting by the door.

"They are cute." Trey tried to smile.

"See." Daren slapped his shoulder.

"Hey guys." The blond bounced toward the truck. The brunet followed, but not so excited.

"Sandy, hi." Daren hugged her.

"This is Abby." She pointed to the other girl.

"This is Trey." He pointed as Trey came around the truck.

"Hi, you're cute." Abby said as she walked over. "I'm pleasantly surprised."

"Nice to meet you to." Trey half smiled wishing this night was over.

They went in and the girls talked nonstop. Trey was looking for an off button, but there was no stopping them. He felt like he was back in high school. They even talked while they were eating, and the laughing, he thought his ears might bleed.

"Well, I'm pretty full." Trey finally said, starting to stand.

"Where are you going?" Daren looked at him like don't leave me behind.

"I need some air."

Daren grabbed the bill laying on the table, and followed. Trey walked outside rubbing his temples.

"You were going to leave me alone with that?" Daren asked as he came out the door.

"You set it up. You should be punished."

"That's nice, glad you got my back."

"Trey!"

Trey turned to see Benton and Shane walking up, and he wanted to hide.

"What are you doing here?" Shane asked, grabbing him and hugging him.

"We are on a date." Daren said.

Benton and Shane looked him up and down.

"Very nice, he is cute." Shane said.

"Yeah, nice to meet you…" Benton said as he went in for a hug.

"I'm Daren." He stammered out, a little shocked by the hug.

"Well, I'm glad to see Trey finally found a man. The four of us will have to go out sometime."

"Uh guys." Trey tried to get them away from Daren.

"Wait, what?" Daren looked all confused.

"It's nothing. We have to go." Trey opened the door and tried to get Benton and Shane to go into the restaurant.

"Hey guys, why are you out here." Sandy said as Abby followed her out.

Now Benton and Shane looked confused.

"Yeah girls, I..."

"It's ok I'll talk to you tomorrow. She needs to get home." The two girls bounced off.

"Trey?" Benton asked.

Trey turned red and walked to the truck. He watched from the truck as Daren, Benton and Shane exchanged a few words. Then Daren got into the truck.

"Is there something you want to tell me?"

"I don't think so."

"Then I have a question for you."

"I don't think I want to hear it."

"Are you gay?"

"Are you sure you want me to answer that?"

"Yes."

Trey sighed and hung his head. "Yes."

"Why didn't you just say so? I would have never asked you to go on this date."

"Well, when I started working with you, I just didn't want any problems, then as we became friends, I wasn't sure how to tell you. Then when you asked about the date, I didn't know what to do."

"You could have told me, I'm fine with it."

"I'm sorry."

He pulled out and they were both quiet the whole way home.

"Again, I'm really sorry." Trey said as he got out.

"I'm fine. We are still friends." Daren smiled at him.

Trey closed the door and headed into the house.

"How'd the date go?" Clayton asked as he headed to the stairs.

"I don't want to talk about it." He headed to his room and to bed.

Chapter Thirty-Four

"Good morning." Daren said as Trey got out of his truck.

"Hey handsome." Valery said as she came out the door.

Trey froze for a moment not sure what Daren had told anyone.

"Listen you over used mattress, neither of us is interested in your worn-out ass."

"You are so rude."

"Why don't you go tell my mom on me?"

She stomped and went back into the house.

"Thanks."

"No worries, I didn't tell anyone anything. Just that those girls were not our type."

"Thank you."

"No one should tell your business. You come out to who you want when you want. Now let's get to work."

Trey was still quiet for a while not sure how Daren was going to be with him, but it seemed nothing had changed. If anything, Daren seemed more playful with him, and he was sure that he was wear more cologne than normal. He put it aside think he must be over thinking it.

"Well, it's lunch, and good news she isn't here. She went with some girlfriends of hers somewhere."

"A peaceful lunch, that is good news."

They all sat in their usual spots and Trey looked at the empty chair across from him and smiled.

"So, I hear the dates didn't go well." Gale asked.

"Definitely not the kind of girl I'm looking for." Trey smiled.

Daren bumped his knee with his knee, and smiled.

"That's good. Don't go and pick just any tramp. Make sure she is right for you."

"Mom don't start." Hunter sighed.

Daren still had his knee pressed up against Treys and was holding it there. Trey kept his knee still; he wasn't about to pull away from him.

Trey worked by himself after lunch. Hunter took Daren with him. Trey was about to get into his truck when Daren came walking over.

"How was your afternoon?"

"It was ok. Yours?"

"I'd rather work with you. He complained about mom picking on Valery all afternoon."

"That must have been fun."

"Yeah, not so much. Are you coming for dinner tonight?"

"No, I have plans with a friend."

"Oh." There was disappointment in his voice.

"Why? What's up?"

"Nothing. Was just thinking maybe we could go for a quad ride again. Hunter doesn't do that much anymore, and it's not as much fun by yourself."

"Well, maybe another day this week."

"Sounds good."

"OK, see you tomorrow."

"See you then."

Trey left confused. Was he hitting on him, or just looking for a guy to pal around with. It was tearing him up inside.

He went home and got cleaned up. Peter had invited him for dinner, and he hadn't seen him since the night he stayed over so he agreed to go.

"Got another date?" Clayton smiled at him.

"No just going to hang out with Peter and Ashley."

"Who is Ashley?"

"His four-year-old. I told you about her."

"Oh yeah, well have fun." Clayton took another bite of his ham sandwich.

Trey got to Peter's place and Peter met him at the door.

"I'm so happy to see you."

"I didn't even knock, where you watching out the window."

"I heard a car and looked out the window. Now get in here." He grabbed his arm and pulled him in.

"Where is Ashley?"

"With mom. I wanted time alone with you."

"I was looking forward to seeing her."

"Well, I don't want to expose her to this yet."

"To what exactly?"

"The gay thing."

"I wasn't planning on doing anything in front of her, nor would I ever."

"I know, it's just that I don't know how I feel about everything, and I don't want to confuse her. I just wanted us to have a romantic dinner."

Trey looked over to see candles on the table and there was soft music playing.

"You seem to know how you feel about me."

"I think I do." He grabbed Trey and planted a kiss on him, but Trey didn't return it right away.

"Is there something wrong?" Peter looked confused.

"No, just surprised is all."

They ate dinner and chatted a little about minor things. Trey helped clean up and then Peter took Trey's hand and led him to the bedroom.

Peter started kissing his neck as he got undressed and it didn't take long for Trey to follow. He grabbed Peter and pushed him on the bed.

"Yeah, that's it be rough with me."

Trey didn't need another invite. It didn't take long for both of them to be done. Trey pulled him in close and lightly kissed his neck. They laid like that for a while.

"I know you have to go home, and I have to go pick up Ashley." Peter finally said.

"I could go with you." Trey offered.

"That's OK, I'm not ready for that yet."

"For what, I have known her since birth." Trey pulled back and looked at him.

"Yeah, but it's different now."

"Whatever." Trey got up and got dressed.

"Don't be mad. We are just friends with benefits."

"I understand that. It's fine I'm not mad." Trey got dressed.

"I'll call you." Peter said as he headed to the door.

"OK." He kissed him lightly and left.

Chapter Thirty-Five

Trey had just gotten home and was getting out of his truck and a truck pulled in behind him.

"Hey Trey."

"Daren, what are you doing here?"

"Can I hang out for a little while? There is a war at home."

"Really?"

They both walked up and sat on the porch step.

"Hunter announced at dinner that he and Valery were getting married."

"What?"

"Mom demanded to know why, and He said because they had to."

"I think we need coffee." Trey headed into the house.

Clayton had coffee already on, and was in the living room watching TV.

"So, mom was like you have to?"

"Shit." Trey sipped his coffee.

"Yeah, turns out she is pregnant."

"Is it his?"

"You sound like my mom. She asked the same question."

"I'm sure she did." Trey almost laughed.

"Don't worry I almost laughed myself. I left before things got worse."

"I'm sure it is war."

"So, I figured I would just hang out with you for a while."

"That's fine with me."

"So, what did you do tonight?"

"I went to see.." Trey stopped not sure what to call Peter right now.

"See what?"

"A friend I guess."

"You guess?"

"Well, it's a long story."

"Did something bad happen?"

"No, just my feelings got a little hurt."

"Sorry to hear that."

"It's OK. I have to go to the barn quick, want to walk along."

"Sure."

They walked down to the barn and Trey checked on the animals and did a few other things.

"Can I ask you a question?" Daren smiled.

"Yeah, ask away."

"When did you realize you were gay?"

Trey looked shocked by the question.

"You can tell me to mind my own business."

"No, it's fine. I guess I knew in high school, but never did anything about it. Tried most of my life to have a girlfriend."

"That didn't make you happy."

"No, I ended up hurting some nice girls. I never wanted to do that."

"So, why did you decide to come out?"

"I had a friend who was very strong and came out. I drew strength from him and decided I needed to be true to myself."

"Well, I'm proud of you for that."

Trey looked at Daren who was smiling at him.

"Why are you asking me all these questions?"

"Just wanted to get to know you more is all."

They walked back up to the house, and Trey's mind was racing with thoughts about why he asked all these questions.

"So how many guys have you been with?"

"Why?" Trey looked confused.

"Just curious."

"That killed the cat you know."

"So, you're not going to answer that."

"No." Trey turned and pushed him on the shoulder.

"Well, if you have never been with a guy how do you know you would like that."

"OK, first I didn't say I had never been with a guy, and second it's about what I'm attracted to."

"So, are you attracted to me?"

"Really?"

"What?"

"No matter how I answer that it's bad."

"What do you mean?"

"If I say yes, you'll be like dude I'm straight back off. If I say no, you'll be like what's wrong with me?"

"I would not."

"Listen I'll see you in the morning." Trey headed up the steps onto the porch.

"So, you're not going to answer." Daren just stood with his arms wide open.

Trey looked at him and smiled devilishly. "No." He turned and headed into the house.

"That was a yes. I knew it." Daren yelled at him as he closed the door.

He locked the door and waited to hear the truck back out and leave. He smiled the whole way to his bedroom.

Chater Thirty-Six

The next several days were very quiet at the farm. Even Daren was not talking.

"Listen, I'm sorry I have been so quiet." Daren said to Trey as he got into his truck to go home.

"It's OK."

"Can I come over later. I really need a break from here."

"Yeah, sure. I'll get something for dinner."

Trey went home and order pizza and grabbed a quick shower. He was paying for the pizza when Daren pulled up.

"I hope pizza is, OK?"

"It's fine." Daren slumped down in a chair at the table.

"Are you OK?"

"Well, everything is so tense at the house. Mom isn't talking to Hunter or Valery. I have never seen her so mad."

"I can feel the tension just working there."

"Mom, keep saying she isn't going to have this tramp owning her farm."

"Ouch." Trey said as he pulled out some paper plates.

"Do you have any beer? I could use a drink."

"Yeah, I have a couple. He pulled them out of the fridge."

"I think mom is going to sell the farm."

"Why?"

"She doesn't want Valery to get any part of it."

"Oh my God."

"I don't know what I'm going to do?"

"Wow, this is worse than, I thought."

"Mom isn't even talking to me."

"Well, if I can help you in any way."

"I may need a place to stay for a while."

"You can stay here anytime you want."

They ate their pizza and drank some more beers, and they ended up setting on the porch.

"I love clear nights like this. You can see so many stars." Trey finished his beer as he looked at the sky.

Daren stood and started to walk.

"Where are you going?"

"I don't know, I don't know anything right now." Daren hung his head and kicked at some stones.

"What do you mean?"

"Things seem to get crazier and crazier. My life isn't what I thought it would be. I was supposed to have a wife by now, maybe a kid on the way. My own little farm."

"Life isn't a life time movie; it doesn't always work out the way we think it should." Trey sighed.

"I know, I'm learning that more and more every day. Things I want I can't have, and it breaks my heart."

"It will work out." Trey walked up and put his hand on his shoulder.

"I don't know."

"You'll find a girl."

"That's not what I want."

"What do you want?"

Daren turned and looked at him with tear filled eyes. He reached up with both hands grabbed his face pulled him in and kissed him gently.

"You."

Trey stood in shock. He couldn't move.

"I'm sorry." Daren said and he turned and went to his truck to leave.

"No, wait." Trey finally got out.

"What?"

"Don't go. You had some drinks, you shouldn't drive."

Trey took his hand and pulled him out of the truck.

"Are you…" Trey wasn't sure how to ask.

"I've known that I'm gay for a long time."

"Does your mom know?"

"I think so, she would never say anything."

Trey pulled Daren in and wrapped his arms around him.

"So, you find me attractive." Trey smiled at him.

"I don't think I want to answer that." Daren smiled back at him.

They finished their beers and went back into the house. Trey led him up the stairs and to his room. They got into bed and Daren crawled in behind Trey and pulled him in close. Trey couldn't believe this was actually happening. The feel of his breath on his neck. His body being pressed up against his, but the beer was having its effect on both of them. The combination of the long hot day and the beer Trey was having a hard time trying to stay awake to enjoy what he had wanted for so long. Then he heard a soft noise in his ear. It was Daren snoring. The long day and beer had taken its toll on him as well.

Chapter Thirty-Seven

The next morning Trey woke and Daren was already gone. He looked at the time and realized he way over slept. He hurried through the shower and finished getting dressed going down the stairs, hoping Daren was waiting for him. He looked around and saw a paper towel with a pen laying on top of it. He had left him a note.

"Sorry I had to go. I hope I didn't hurt you last night. I shouldn't have done what I did. We will talk later."

He laid the towel down on the table. "What does that mean?" Trey said as his mind ran in a million different directions. His fast pace now slowed as he wasn't sure he even wanted to go to work now.

"What if he doesn't like me like that?" Trey muttered to himself.

"There is only one way to find out." Came a voice from behind him. He turned to see his mom standing there.

"Mom, when did you get home?" He ran to her and hugged her.

"An hour or so ago. Daren was leaving as I was pulling in."

"Oh."

"Imagine my surprise, then I saw the note."

"I'm sorry."

"Nothing to be sorry about. Do you like him."

Trey looked to see what answer she was looking for and found nothing.

"Yes."

"So, what happen last night?"

"Are you sure you want to know?"

"No, but tell me anyway."

"Things at his house are crazy, and he came over for pizza and some beer. He ended up kissing me. We went to my room and both passed out before anything happened. I came down to this note."

"And you're not sure what it means?"

"No, I'm not."

"I see. Well, I'm only here to get the rest of my things." She walked over to the coffee pot.

"Wait, what?" Trey was confused.

"Yes, I found a lovely nursing home. I'm staying in a small apartment. I can come and go as I wish. There are people there my age that I can socialize with. You don't need me here anymore."

"Of course I do."

She looked at him and smiled. "I love you very much, as I do your brothers. I just can't stay here. I miss your father so much, and everything around here reminds me of him. It's just so hard."

"I understand."

"I'm only a phone call away. Clayton and Eddie are in and out of here all the time to. You won't be alone."

"I'm going to miss having you here." He hugged her.

"I'll come visit I promise."

"So, are you going to help me with my problem before you go?"

"No."

"No?"

"Because I'm not the one you need to talk to. I don't have the answers you're looking for."

Trey sighed heavy.

"I will say when people are drinking the things that hold them back fade away, and they tend to be more open and say how they feel."

"OK."

"That also doesn't mean they won't bury those feelings for whatever reason when they are sober."

"You're right, you're not much help." He smiled at her. "I have to go."

"I will be gone when you get back. Take the master room now, this is your place." She walked over and hugged him.

"Thank you, mom."

"I know you will make your dad proud." She kissed his forehead, and Trey left. A lot of emotions running through him and he found he had tears in his eyes.

"You're late." Daren said as he got out of his truck.

"My mom showed up this morning."

"I saw her pulling in when I was leaving. Is everything OK?"

"She is moving into a nursing home. It's just too much for her at the farm."

"I'm sorry."

"No, it's OK. It's one where she can come and go as she wants. She will be around people her own age, so she is happy."

"Well, that's good. I have started the cows. Come help me finish."

He followed Daren to the barn.

"Where is everyone?"

"Mom went into town early. She said she won't be back till around dinner time. She left us sandwiches for lunch. Hunter went for part for the baler again, and Valery went shopping for baby things."

"I see, so it's just us."

"Yep." Daren went about taking care of the cows. Trey didn't know what to say, so he said nothing and went to work. As they worked, he could swear that Daren was looking him up and down, checking him out, but he wasn't saying anything. It was driving him nuts. They were just finishing cleaning the equipment and Daren walked up behind him.

"Follow me." He whispered in his ear. His breath on his neck almost sent him over the edge.

They walked out behind the barn. Daren stopped on a dime, turned and was face to face with Trey.

"I'm sorry about last night." Daren smiled at him.

"I'm going to need you to specify what you're talking about." Trey smiled.

"Falling asleep." Daren looked at him weird then realized what he was thinking. He smiled grabbed him by the collar pulled him in and kissed him, and left him go. "I think I am falling in love with you."

"I am so happy."

"I feel like a weight has been lifted. I have never told anyone that I am gay."

"I know it's tough."

Daren leaned in again and kissed him. Trey grabbed him by the neck and kissed him deeply.

"What was that?" Daren said as he pulled away.

"I'm not sure."

"Guys!"

They came around the barn and saw Valery yelling for them.

"What are you to doing back there?"

"One of the cats were stuck in a hole again. Trey helped me get it free."

"Oh."

"You're back early."

"Yeah, I'm not feeling good. I'm going to lay down." She turned and went into the house.

"You don't think she suspects anything do you?" Trey asked.

"I don't know. I hope not. Let's get the rest of the work done."

They skipped lunch and finished their work early.

"Come back later. We will take the quads out."

"OK, sounds fun."

Trey went home and couldn't wait to get back over to see Daren. His mother left him a note.

"I'm glad you're happy. I hope it works out for you and Daren. Love you mom." He smiled and laid it down. He grabbed a quick bite to eat and headed back over to see Daren.

"I'm in the barn." Daren yelled as Trey got out of the truck.

Trey smiled and almost skipped to the barn.

"You ready to go?"

"Yes."

Trey followed Daren and they went through fields and mud pits. They road for over half hour and ended up by a small pond.

"Why are we stopping?" Trey asked as Daren got off his quad.

"Come here." He motioned for Trey to come to him.

"What?" Trey asked as he stood in front of him.

"I want you. I want to make you mine." He grabbed Trey under his jaw and pulled him in a kissed him. He turned his head sideways and started kissing his neck. "Take your shirt off." He whispered in his ear as he let him go.

Trey took his shirt off quickly. His hairy chest glistening in the sun. Daren ran his hands through his thick chest hair and then grabbed it and pulled him in close. He was kissing him all over his chest.

"Oh God don't stop." Trey whispered.

Daren spun around behind him and grabbed his neck from behind pulled him back into him.

"I have been wanting to do this for a while now." Daren whispered again. Before Trey knew what was happening, Daren had his pants undone and around his ankles. He pushed him over the seat of the quad. He felt him probe with his fingers.

"I have never done this before." Trey said a little scared.

"I'll take it easy." Daren said as he spit in his hand. Daren navigated his way in, and at first the pain was almost more than he could take, but then it turned to pleasure at he was hitting the right spot.

"Oh my God." Trey heard himself say.

"Can I go harder?"

"Please."

Daren started pounding him harder and harder. Trey had never felt anything like this. He didn't want it to end. Daren pulled out and grabbed him by the shoulder and pulled him up straight.

"Why did you stop?"

"Step out of those pants." Daren told him, and Trey did so. Daren led him around the bush that was in front of him and on the ground by the pond was a blanket and two beach towels.

"Lay on your back." Daren told him.

Trey did so and Daren put Trey's legs in the air and was deep inside him in seconds. He looked Trey right in the eyes as he continued to punish his hole. Trey reached up and grabbed him by the neck, pulling him in for a kiss. After for what seemed a long time, they finished, and they both just laid on the blanket.

"Did you like that?" Daren smiled at him. They both laid there their hair chest covered in sweat.

"I did."

"Me to." Daren rolled on his side and just looked at Trey.

"What?" Trey smiled at him.

"I just never in a million years thought this would happen. You have made me very happy."

"I'm very happy to."

"I want us to..." Daren stopped and laid back.

"I would like that to. Let's just take our time and see how it goes." Trey finished knowing what he was thinking.

Daren smiled and him and a goofy smile came over his face.

"Last one in the pond is bottom next time." Daren slapped Trey's chest and darted into the pond.

"Not fair." Trey protested lightly. He enjoyed being the bottom. He ran into the pond and the two splashed and dunked each other.

Chapter Thirty-Eight

Trey got home; he was happier than he had been in a long time. He heard a car coming and looked back. It was Valery. He took a deep breath.

"Well looks like you had a fun evening."

"What do you want?"

"Just came to see how the hero is doing."

"Hero?"

"Well, you did save that cat today."

"Cat?" Trey looked confused.

"You know behind the barn."

"Oh yeah. What about it?"

"Wow, do you rescue so many animals that you don't remember that one?"

"Did you come over for a reason or to just be weird."

"Seems we are all acting a little weird these days."

"We?"

"Well, mine could be because of hormones. Not sure what your reason is."

"I don't have time for games. Is there something you need?" Trey was annoyed now.

"Just want you to know your secret is safe with me."

"What secret?"

"Well, for now anyway."

"OK, I'm going into my house. You can go home."

"However, it does explain why you keep turning me down."

Trey froze. She must have seen them kissing. This could end badly. He slowly turned back to her.

"I'm not sure what you think you know, but I'm sure it's not what you think." Trey walked back down the steps trying to intimidate her.

"Oh, honey I know. Listen as soon as we get married that means you're working for me."

"Oh, you didn't know. I'm done there in a week and a half."

"I'll make sure you stick around."

Both their phones went off at the same time.

"Hunter says his mom wants me home." She said confused.

"Odd, Daren said his mom needs me to come over."

They just looked at each other. She got in her car and left. Trey went to the house and locked his door again and headed to his truck.

Trey knocked on the door when he got there. He had checked the time and it was nine, seemed rather late to him.

"Come in Trey, come to the kitchen." Gale's voice ran through the house.

Trey walked into the kitchen where Gale, Hunter, Valery and Daren were waiting.

"Now that everyone is here. I want to say I am taking control again."

"What are you talking about mom?" Hunter looked annoyed.

"Hunter, you have made some bad decisions lately that are affecting this family in a negative way. I can no longer stand by and do nothing."

"He is a good man." Valery started.

"You are one of those mistakes." Gale shut her down.

"So, what is it you want mom?" Hunter asked.

"The first mistake was leasing those two fields. I told you to just buy the hay as we needed, it would be cheaper that way, but no you wouldn't listen."

"Mom."

"I am taking charge." She put her hand up and Hunter shut up. "Now, I talked to my lawyer today and we drew up this contract to get out of the lease." She handed it to Trey. He looked at it.

"It states you will let me out of the lease in exchange for all my livestock and a few pieces of machinery to be named by you."

"Mom, are you crazy?" Hunter exploded.

"I am selling the farm Hunter. I will not have this piece of trash getting anything from me."

"You'll understand if I want my lawyer to take a look at this first?" Trey could not believe what was going on.

"Of course. I have a buyer already for the rest of the farm."

"Where will we live?" Hunter's anger was almost out of control.

"I don't care where you and this slut live. I have also redone my will. Hunter as long as you have anything to do with her, you will receive nothing."

"What?"

"Daren, as for you. I know what has been going on here." She pointed to the two of them. "While his mother may not care about his soul. I care about yours. You will not receive anything from me until you are married and have a child."

Daren and Trey just looked at each other confused. How did she know.

"I saw you leave with the blanket and towel; I knew you were going by the pond. I drove up the road and walked down the path and waited. I have known for a long time that you were leaning that way. It's not worth your soul baby."

"What is she talking about." Hunter exploded.

"Daren and Trey are seeing each other." Valery blurted out.

"What?!"

"I'm not done with you yet either." She turned to Valery.

"Remember I'm with child. Don't upset me."

"Really, and what doctor did you go to?"

"Our family doctor."

"That's interesting. I talked to them today, they said you were not in at all last week. In fact, I check with several urgent cares and hospitals and no one has seen you."

Valery looked scared and just looked back and forth between Hunter and his mother.

"You bitch you ruined everything." Valery took a step toward her.

Hunter grabbed her arm, and spun her around to face him.

"So, you're not pregnant?"

"No, not that it matters now. You lost everything."

His mother stepped up and slapped her across the face so hard that Trey and Daren jumped back.

"How dare you. Get out of my house now."

Valery stood there holding her face in shock.

"You were only after me for my money?" Hunter was still piecing everything together. Valery didn't answer just turned and stomped away.

"Now I am buying a ranch style house in Sandy valley. Daren you are going to live there with me."

"That's so far away." Daren said.

"This family has embarrassed itself and we need to move away."

"What about me?" Hunter asked.

"Depends on what you decided."

He looked back to see Valery coming down the stairs with bags in her hands.

"I love her." Hunter said looking back at his mother.

"Then you are on your own." She put her hand up to stop him from saying anything. He huffed and followed her out the door.

"I will make arrangements to have everything delivered to you. Now if you don't mind Daren and I need to start packing." She pointed toward the door, and Trey knew it was time to leave.

Trey walked outside as Valery was yelling at Hunter.

"Yes, I lied. It's the only way you would marry me. Now you have nothing to offer."

"But I love you. We can make it work."

"You must be joking. We are done. You're just a broke loser now." She got into her car and slammed the door. Hunter stumbled off to the barn in tears. She sped out the drive way and Trey followed her out.

Chapter Thirty-Nine

Trey got home and tears were flowing freely. Only a couple hours ago he was the happiest he has been in a long time, now everything was a train wreck. He laid the paper on the table, and stumbled up the stairs to his room.

He tried to sleep, but his heart was breaking so bad he couldn't stop crying. At some point he fell asleep.

"Trey my boy."

Trey's eyes blinked, and things were blurry.

"Trey, can you hear me?"

"Dad?"

"Yes, my boy."

"Am I dead?" Trey opened his eyes wide, and looked around. He was in the barn, with everything that was there before he died.

"How?"

"I brought you here."

"Dad, things are crazy right now."

"I see that."

"My heart is broke."

"So, you're going to give up?"

"What?"

"You know gay relationships aren't so different from straight."

"What do you mean?"

"I wasn't good enough for your mother. Her dad forbid her to see me. We went behind his back for months."

"Really?"

"Yes, He came around, and we had a good relationship."

"I'm really falling for him."

"What about Peter?"

"That was never supposed to happen, and he only wants me for a quicky and that's it."

"Seems you know what you want."

"Dad."

"What?"

"Am I making you proud."

"Always, you are a strong man. Be proud of yourself."

"I'm getting tired."

"It's time for me to go."

"I miss you so much dad."

"I miss you. We will be together again one day, but you have a lot to accomplish before that. Tell your mom I love and miss her."

Trey didn't get a chance to answer before he was asleep.

He woke and it was morning. His eyes were all puffy and hurt from crying. He got up and went downstairs and made coffee. He sat quietly drinking coffee until there was a knock at the door.

"Go away."

"Trey it's me." Valery said. "We need to talk."

Trey sighed and walked toward the door.

"Listen I think we should work together to get our men back, and what belongs to them."

"I'm not sure why you think I want anything to do with you."

"I'm hurt."

"Really, you lie and manipulate people and you wonder why."

"Listen I put several years into getting that, I deserve something."

"Do you hear yourself?"

"Trey are you OK?" Benton and Shane came flying in the house.

"Yes, why." Trey and Valery were caught off guard.

"You don't know do you?" Shane looked at him.

"Know what?"

"Hunter. He um…" Benton stopped unable to finished.

"What about Hunter?" Valery looked at them.

"He is gone." Shane sighed.

"Where did he go?" Valery asked not understanding.

"What happen?" Trey asked ignoring her.

"After she left, he must have felt he lost everything." Benton started.

"What I heard from my friend on the ambulance is that he hung himself in the barn." Shane said in a low tone.

"What, how is he?" Valery still couldn't process everything.

"He is gone!" Trey yelled at her.

"But." She started.

"You used him and left him. You pushed him to this." Trey continued to yell at her.

"I didn't think he loved me that much."

"You played with his heart! You did this!" Trey yelled again.

"Trey." Benton put his hand on his shoulder.

"Honey, why don't you come outside with me." Shane grabbed her hand and led her outside.

"Are you sure about this?" Trey felt like he might be sick.

"I'm sorry, yes."

Tears flowed now. He had become close to the whole family and couldn't believe how everything was falling apart.

"This isn't the guy from the restaurant, is it?"

"No, it's his older brother."

Valery left and Shane came back into the house.

"She said she needed to go see her friends."

Trey looked at both of them, and explained everything from the night before.

"Wow, that is messed up." Benton shook his head.

"You two make a cute couple." Shane offered.

As the morning wore on, more cars came. Trey's mother finally showed up.

"I was over and talked to his mother. She is a mess, and so is Daren. He pulled me aside and asked about you. He said he will contact you soon, to wait to hear from him."

"Thanks mom."

They hugged, as Stan and the family pulled in.

Chapter Forty

Trey walked into Hunter's funeral service. He could see Daren and his mother sitting up front. Both their eyes were swollen from crying. Daren noticed him and darted to him.

"Oh my God. I'm so sorry." Trey said as they hugged.

"We thought he left with her." He sobbed into Trey's shoulder.

Trey didn't know what to say, just continued to hug him.

"I found him the next morning when I went to the barn." Daren continued without lifting his head.

"I'm so sorry." He continued to rub his back.

"Thank you for coming." Gale walked up, and pulled Daren off of him.

"I'm so sorry for your loss."

"Thank you." She was not as friendly with him as she had always been. Seeing them together had changed her attitude toward him.

"My dear, I'm so sorry." Anna came around him and hugged her.

Daren grabbed Trey's hand and pulled him aside.

"How are you handling everything?" Trey asked as they sat down.

"I'm not good. I wish I could spend time with you." Daren sighed and hung his head.

"I really want to be with you." Trey took his hands.

"I know, but I can't, I mean I was going to tell her that all I needed was you. Then this happened. I can't do that to her, not right now anyway."

"I understand." Trey noticed a hand on Daren's shoulder.

"We have other people here to see us. We need to greet them." Gale said, and Daren stood turned and walked toward the front, His mother stepped in front of Trey."

"I expect to have a signed contract within two days. We are moving."

"I will have it there."

"You know, it's not that I don't like you. I do. You're hard working and know what you are doing. I'm sure you will run your farm very well."

Trey looked confused not sure where this was going.

"I just don't approve of the way you chose to live your life, and I won't let you drag my son down with you."

Trey was ready to explode. He really hated when people called it a choice. It's just what he is attracted to. He didn't choose that any more than a guy chooses to be attracted to a girl.

"If I had a daughter, I would be thrilled for you to date her. I hope you understand." She smiled at him, turned and walked away without waiting for a response.

Trey just stood there and looked as others came to console the two. Daren looked so depressed on so many levels, and he could do nothing at the moment to help. It broke his heart. He turned and headed out the door.

"Trey." A voice came from behind him. He turned to see his uncle Chris standing there.

"I'm so sorry. Are you ok?"

"No." Tears flowed freely.

"Want to talk?"

"Not really. I just want to be alone."

"I'm here if you need me."

"Thank you." Trey turned and went to his truck. He headed home and went to the barn, took care of the animals to try and get things off his mind. He soon found himself sitting in the hay loft crying again.

"I figured this is where you were." Chris said as he climbed up.

"I just need to be alone."

"Alone is not good, get to much into your head. You'll make yourself crazy."

"I don't know what to do right now."

"Your mother is worried about you."

"Tell her I am ok."

"You want me to lie to her?"

"A little white lie."

"I don't think I can do that."

"What do you want from me?"

"For you to listen."

"Fine I'm listening." Trey wiped away his tears and tried to sit up straight.

"Years ago, I fell in love with a guy. I knew I would never find anyone else that I loved as much. We always had the best time together. Then due to circumstances out of my control we were separated."

"I remember the story."

"Let me continue."

"Sorry."

"We were both made to believe, that what we were was a sin, and God hated us. I spent a lot of time praying that how I felt would change, and nothing. I thought maybe God didn't love me. I mean my family didn't why should he? We both let events and others control our lives."

"I just don't know what to do."

"Do you think God makes mistakes."

"No." Trey was remembering his talk with Jeramy now.

"Which do you think God thinks is worse murder or swearing?"

"Murder of course."

"No, all sin is equal to him. No one sin is any worse than another."

"Really."

"We are the ones who have to rank things so we can justify ourselves. Well at least I didn't murder anyone, we tell ourselves when we curse."

"So, what are you telling me?"

"Take charge don't let others determine your future. You determine. Don't let others judge you, that is for God to do."

"How do I do that?"

"You're a smart boy. You'll figure it out. Just don't waste your life, you never want to look back and say what if I had done this or that. I do that all the time and it's not a good feeling."

"Thank you." He leaned over and hugged him.

"Now, the first thing is to stop crying and come into the house. Your mother made me go shopping so she could make dinner. Just so you know she was appalled at the amount of junk food and lack of good food to make for dinner."

"No worries, I'll blame Clayton." Trey smiled a little as he got up.

"To late he already blamed you."

Trey hung his head and laughed a little as they headed down the ladder.

Chapter Forty-One

Two days later Trey found himself standing in front of Daren's house. He had the signed contract in his hands, that were shaking. He had decided he was going to talk to her about everything. There were cattle trailers already loaded and two empty ones. He walked toward the house and she met him at the door.

"Good morning, Miss Stone." Trey said as he walked up.

"Good morning, Trey. I assume you signed the contract."

"I did. I talked to my lawyer, he said it wasn't a bad deal." He handed her the paper.

"You picked the equipment you wanted?"

"Yes, it's all in there."

"Fine then I will have everything delivered today."

"Miss Stone." Trey looked at her and he almost ran fearing how she might react to what he had to say.

"Is there something you wish to say."

"No." Trey started to chicken out.

"Very well then." She turned to go back into the house.

"Actually, yes there is." Trey said forcing himself to stand his ground.

"Very well, what is it you have to say?" She turned to face him.

"I love Daren, from the first time I met him all I could think about was him. I know you think it's a sin and you want to save his soul. I don't think God makes mistakes. I have prayed many times over the years that things would be different, but that has never changed for me. I figured if God loves me the way I am then I should love me as well. It took a long time to come to terms with that and to come out to my family. I also realized everyone sins, and it doesn't matter if it's cursing or killing, in Gods eyes a sin is a sin. God is the only one who should be judging. Not you, not me, not even the pope. We are called to love each other, weather we agree with the person or not. I will be right here waiting for Daren and I hope you love him enough to do the right thing." Trey stopped feeling like he might be sick.

"Are you quite finished?"

Trey thought for a second. "Yes, ma'am I am. Have a good day." Trey turned to leave and Daren was standing there with a shocked look on his face. Behind him he heard the front door close.

"Oh, um Daren. I didn't know you were there." Trey wasn't sure how much he heard.

"I heard everything." Daren just smiled at Trey.

"I meant it all."

"I believe you did."

"Maybe I should be going." Trey said as he walked past him toward his truck.

"Trey."

"Yes." Trey turned to look at Daren.

"I love you to."

Trey's heart almost stopped. He tried to say something, but nothing came out.

"I have to take some time with mom. She is hurting right now." Daren smiled at him.

"I understand."

Daren looked at the house then back to Trey.

"I need to go check on her. You gave her some pretty hard truth."

"I'm sorry." Trey didn't know what else to say.

"Don't be. I wish I had said it." He smiled and walked to the house.

Trey turned and went to his truck, wishing he had at least got one last hug. He drove the short distance home, all mixed up and confused.

A couple hours later trucks started pulling in with the livestock and machinery. It took the better part of the day to get everything into place.

Trey kept looking hoping Daren would show up on one of the trucks but he didn't. As the last truck was getting unloaded one of the drivers came up to Trey.

"Are you Trey?"

"Yes."

"I'm supposed to give this to you."

He handed him a letter. It smelled like Daren; he had put some of his cologne on it. He opened it and read it.

"I left you the two quads. Keep them I will be back to go for a ride with you. I love you. I need some time right now. I hope you will wait for me. Love Daren."

"Where do you want the quads?" The man asked as he was bringing the first off.

"Over here in the barn." Trey said as he held the letter to his chest.

Chapter Forty-Two

Two weeks later Trey was in his kitchen and there was a knock at the door.

"Come in." He yelled as he was busy at the stove.

"What are you doing." Benton said as he and Shane came in.

"Making lunch for the guys."

"What guys?"

"Well, I was having trouble finding help. So, I went to the FFA at the high school to see if they knew anyone, and they have a program where seniors can take half the day and work the job they want and the other they do school work on line. So, I got two seniors working here in the mornings, they come in for lunch do school work after lunch for a couple hours, then go back to work."

"That's amazing." Shane shook his head.

"Yeah, way to think outside the box."

"Thanks, they have been here a week and are working out great."

"Do you have to pay them?" Shane asked as he sat down.

"I do, but I get some of that back from the school district."

"Nice. Listen we stopped by to see if you wanted to go out for dinner. I know with everything lately you have been busy."

"I would like that."

"How about Smoky bones. I love that place." Benton said.

"I haven't been there in forever let's go." Trey smiled.

"We will pick you up around six." Shane said as he stood.

"See you then."

Trey smiled as they left and the boys entered looking very hungry. Later Trey was waiting for them to pick him up.

"We are going home now." One of the boys yelled through the screen door.

"OK, boys see you tomorrow." Trey smiled and he saw Benton and Shane pulling in. He went out to meet them, locking the door behind him.

They made small talk on the way to the restaurant, Trey was starting to feel better. The past couple of weeks had been hard. He missed Daren a lot, he thought he would have contacted him by now. He hadn't talked to Peter much still bothered by the whole not wanting him to be around his daughter. This night was just what he needed.

They got to the restaurant and got seated quickly to their surprise.

"Wow not to terribly busy." Trey smiled.

"Hi, I'm Quin, I'll be your server tonight."

The three of them looked up to see a tall dark Hispanic man with chiseled features looking back at them. His smile made all three of them take pause. They all gave the once over before looking at each other.

"So, what can I get you gentlemen to drink tonight?'

"Pepsi." Benton choked out first.

"Me to." Shane and Trey said at the same time.

"Ok, I'll be right back with those." He smiled again and left.

"Did you see his..." Benton started.

"Yes. Holy shit." Trey smiled.

"Definitely Pick the right place to come to."

Quin walked past them carrying food to another table and they all three followed him with their eyes. He went to a table where two couples sat.

"Oh, no It can't be." Trey's tone changed.

"What?" Benton was confused.

"That' bitch is hanging all over that guy."

"Who?" Shane asked as Trey stood.

Quin walked away from the table and Trey slowly walked over.

"Nice to see you are so happy." Trey said as he walked up.

"What?" A blond haired well build guy asked him. The girl with him was quiet.

"Do you know what you're getting yourself into buddy?" Trey looked at the guy.

"What are you talking about. I'm just on a date with my girlfriend."

"Girlfriend, that didn't take long."

"Shut up and go away." The girl on the other side of the table said.

"Yeah, mind your own business." Valery chimed in.

"You manipulated and destroyed a guy to the point that he took his own life, and he happen to be a friend of mine, so it is my business."

"What are you talking about?" The guy looked totally confused.

"It's nothing." Valery rubbed her hand on the guy's chest and gave Trey the dirty looks.

"Nothing!" Trey slammed his hands on the table. Causing everyone to look and Benton and Shane to stand and head his way.

"Listen buddy I don't know what your problem is, but we can take this outside if you like." The guy started to stand.

"This right here." Trey pointed at Valery. "Lied to my friends said she was pregnant, knowing he would marry her, just so she could get his money. When his mother made sure that wouldn't happen, she called him a looser and left him so broken hearted he killed himself. That was two weeks ago."

The guy looked at her confused.

"Baby we went on our first date almost two weeks ago. This can't be true."

"You went on a date right away!" Trey wanted to hit her, but restrained himself.

"He was a loser." Valery finally said.

"You said you didn't care about my money, that you didn't even know I had money." The guy said now backing away from her.

"I told you something was off about these two." The other guy at the table stood now.

"Don't listen to him. Babe, I love you." Valery started to say.

"Me or my money?"

"Can't a girl love both?" She smiled at him.

"Come Bret we are out of here." The two guys started to walk out.

"But you're our ride." Valery protested.

"Sucks to be you." He said and kept walking.

"What the hell are you doing sticking your nose in my business?" Valery yelled at him, as a manager started walking toward them.

"You caused a lot of hurt in people I care about. I won't let you do that again."

"You know he wasn't even that good in bed. Probably just another faggot like you." Valery said grabbing a glass of water and throwing it in his face.

"I'm afraid I'm going to have to asked all of you to leave." The manager said as he walked up.

"Gladly." Valery and her friend stormed off.

"I'm going." Trey said to the manager. He walked over to Benton and Shane. "I'm sorry guys."

"It's fine. We can go somewhere else to eat." Benton said.

"Can we have the check for the drinks?" Shane asked the manager.

"Just go."

They left and got in the car.

"Dude, I thought you were going to lay her out." Shane shook his head.

"When you slammed the table. I thought here we go a bar fight." Benton half laughed.

"I really wanted to lay her out. What a bitch."

"I will never understand how some people can be so heartless. She was the one at your house the morning he was found?" Shane looked back at Trey.

"Yes, I guess when she went to see her friend, they went man hunting."

"Let's just have a nice dinner and forget about her. I will say though I am proud to have you as a friend." Benton smiled back at him as they pulled into the Texas roadhouse.

"I bet the waiter here isn't going to be anywhere near as hot." Trey smiled.

They laughed and headed into the restaurant.

Chapter Forty-Three

The farm kept Trey busy so he didn't think about Daren or anything else. He would eat early and go to bed; during the day he was catching up on the things around the farm he had let slide. The two kids he hired were doing a great job and he needed to do less. Then one after noon he was sitting in his kitchen with nothing to do. He looked at his phone and realized it had been almost a month since the incident at the restaurant.

"If you miss him call him." A voice said as it entered the house. He looked up to see his mother standing there.

"Mom, it's so good to see you." He sprinted to her and gave her a hug.

"I love you to." She hugged him back.

"What are you doing here?"

"Well, Clayton and Eddie said you are working yourself to death instead of dealing with your feelings."

"They said that?" Trey looked weird at her knowing they would never say anything like that.

"Well, not in those words, but that's what they meant." She smiled and went to get herself a cup of coffee. "So, tell me what's going on."

"I'm just lonely."

"Then do something about it."

Trey looked at his mother and smiled. "I know you're right."

"I'm always right." She smiled back.

Trey looked around thinking, then noticed a suitcase by the door.

"Are you moving in?"

"Thanksgiving is in a week. Everyone is coming here. So, if you don't mind me staying, I want to get things ready."

"I would love it. You can have your room; I'll stay in my old room."

"You don't have to…"

"No, I insist." He grabbed her suitcase and took it upstairs.

"Thank you." She said as he came back into the kitchen.

"I really need to go to town for a few things, do you need anything?"

"Funny you should ask. Here." She handed him a notebook page full of stuff, and her bank card.

"I can pay for this."

She just gave him a look that told him not to argue.

"I'll be back shorty; the guys will probably be finished before I get back. There pay is laying on the counter."

"Oh, yes. Very nice boys. I met them when I pulled up."

Trey smiled and left. He was very happy to have her home, even if it was for a short time.

Trey went to Tractor supply to pick up a few things he needed. He decided to stop by and see Peter. He hadn't talk to him in quite sometime, and maybe he would want to get together. He was feeling very lonely, and friends with benefits was better that nothing.

He walked into Peter's shop and stopped not believing who he saw there.

"Valery? What are you doing here?" Trey slowly said.

"Oh, hey. I'm just meeting my new boyfriend." She flashed and evil smile.

"What?" Trey was confused.

"Oh, Trey. Good you met my new girlfriend." Peter smiled as he walked over.

"Your what?" Trey couldn't believe what he was hearing.

"Yeah, we met a couple of weeks ago. I think we have spent every day together since." Valery smiled at him again.

"And Ashley just loves her." Peter smiled.

"Wait." Trey put his hand up.

"Oh, that's the phone excuse me." Peter turned and walked away.

"What are you doing?" Trey demanded.

"Well, you ruined my new boyfriend for me. So, I went on Facebook and looked through your friends and after a little digging he seems to be the closest of your friends, I intend to ruin that for you."

"You are truly insane."

"You being tied up with work or whatever for a couple of weeks has only helped me. Thank you."

"This won't work."

"Oh, he is so desperate this is a cake walk."

"Honey, I'm going to go check on Ashley for you." She turned smiled and walked away.

"So, what do you think?" Peter asked as he walked up to Trey.

"Listen to me, she is not the one."

"I know her past, with Hunter and what happen. It's seems to me the mother is more to blame."

"She is bad news."

"She said you didn't like her much. You just need to get to know her better is all."

Trey sighed not sure what to say.

"Listen we are still friends, but the benefits are over. I think she is the one, just be happy for me."

"I'm here for you." Trey tried to smiled as anger built up inside of him.

"Thanks, I knew I could count on you."

Trey left trying to control the anger he was feeling knowing she would only hurt him in the end. He walked down the street to a small coffee shop, ordered a coffee and sat down and sipped at his coffee.

"Is this seat taken?" A voice came and Trey looked up in shock.

"Um, oh no, please sit, um." Trey was searching for his name but his mind was blank.

"Quin." He said and sat down across the table from him. He was wearing a tight t-shirt that showed every muscle. His blue jeans didn't hide much either.

"How are you?" Trey asked not knowing what else to say.

"I'm good. Do you remember me from smokey bones, I started to wait on you and your friends before you left."

"I do." Trey was a little embarrassed now. "I'm sorry for how I acted that night." Trey had his head down.

"From what I could hear she deserved it."

Trey looked at him now. His chiseled face smiling at him.

"What are you doing in this area?"

"Well, I live here and go to Bloomsburg University."

"I see, little bit of a drive to go to work."

"I worked at a smokey bones at home just transferred for school."

"Oh." Trey didn't know what else to say.

"I don't want to offend you, but I noticed you checking me out that night."

Trey's face turned beat red. "No, I…"

"It's ok. I liked it."

Trey's mind was racing, what was happening here. Is this guy hitting on him. That couldn't be.

"Listen, I have always had a think for rugged farm guys." Quin continued.

"What?" Trey stammered.

"I was hoping to run into you again, I didn't expect it to be here. I figured it would be at work."

"What?" Trey said again thinking this has to be a dream.

"I mean if you're not seeing anyone, maybe we could go out sometime."

"You want to go on a date with me?"

"Unless you're involved with someone. I don't mean to be this forward, but I'm lonely and it's not easy finding a guy like you."

"With me?" Trey thought his heart might stop at any minute.

"If you don't want to. It's fine." He started to get up.

"NO, no." Trey grabbed his hand, and he sat back down.

"Then you want to go on a date?" He smiled at him.

"Yes."

"I'm off tomorrow night. I'm on my way to work right now."

"Ok."

He pulled a pen from his pocket and grabbed Trey's hand. "This is my number. Text me I'll pick you up."

"OK." Trey smiled.

"Can I get a hug before I go?"

"Yes!" Trey almost jumped from his seat. He was taller than Trey so he bent down and hugged him.

"I'm looking forward to getting to know you." He whispered in his ear, then kissed him softly on the cheek. "I'll see you tomorrow." He said as he turned and left.

Trey sat slowly down in the chair and after he was out the door, Trey grabbed his phone a quickly put his number in and texted him. This is Trey.

He texted back. Until tomorrow.

Chapter Fourty-Four

The next day went by slowly as he worked with the guys in the barn. They asked him several times if he was OK. He just smiled and said yes. He was glad his mom had went shopping then was going to his brother's house and wouldn't be home till late. He didn't want to talk about the date with anyone, he was afraid he would jinx it.

He came down the stairs wearing nice clothes, he had put on his silver chain, that he only wore on special occasions. He put twice as much cologne on as usual, he kept smelling himself.

"I think I put too much on." He said as he sniffed himself again.

"To much what?"

He looked to see his mother and Stan walking in.

"Oh, hey you're back earlier than I expected."

"I see." She smiled at him.

"You must have a hot date." Stan smiled at him.

"Um." He looked down at himself and was trying to think of what he should say.

"The dating necklace is a dead giveaway." His mother smiled at him.

"Who's the lucky guy?" Stan said as he sat a bag on the table.

"Well..." He still didn't know what to say.

"He must be very cute. You do have a lot of cologne on." His mother said as she kissed his cheek.

"Should I go shower again?" He said as he turned toward the steps.

"I didn't say it was too much. Just more than you normally do."

"Do I look OK?" He held his arms out and spun around.

"You look great." Stan reassured him.

"So, I take it, it's just me and Stan for dinner." She laughed, as a horn honked outside.

"Ah, he is here. Do we get to meet him?" Stan headed toward the door followed by his mother.

"Do I have a choice?"

"No." His mother said without looking back.

"Hi." Quin said as he got out of the car and looked confused.

"Hi." Trey said as he pushed past his mother and Stan.

"Hi, I'm Trey's mother and you are?"

"I'm Quin. Nice to meet you."

"I'm Stan his older brother." Stan waved.

"Hi." Quin smiled back.

"Ok, well we are going to get going now." Trey got into Quin's car.

"They seem nice." Quin said as he got back in.

"Give it time." Trey smiled at him.

"It's family's job to try and embarrass you." Quin smiled and took Trey's hand in his hand, interlocking their fingers.

Trey felt a calming flow through him as he held his hand. Quin back the car up and headed out the drive way.

"Where are we going?" Trey asked.

"There is a little diner I know. I thought it would be a nice place to get to know each other."

"Sounds nice."

They pulled into a small diner, and soon were eating dinner.

"So, tell me a little about yourself." Trey smiled at him

"Well, I grew up in Portland Oregon. I was an only child; my dad was a drunk and mom left him when I was young. My mom passed away from cancer a couple years ago. I promised her I would finish college, so I got a scholarship to Bloom, so here I am."

"Wow, you're a strong guy handling all of that."

"Well, you do what you have to. What about you."

"My dad just passed; it's been hard. We were close. I am fortunate. I have my mom and three brothers for support."

"Three brothers, where do you fall?"

"I'm the youngest."

"Aww the baby of the family. That's nice."

Trey just smiled at him.

"I have always had a thing for farms, and farm boys." Quin smiled at him.

"How did you know I was gay?" Trey asked the question he had been wanting to ask all night.

"You were checking me out that night at the restaurant. You didn't hide it at all."

"I have got to work on that?" Trey blushed a little.

"It was fine. I enjoyed it." He took Trey's hand and squeezed it.

Trey smiled back

"Will there be anything else gentlemen?" The waitress asked as she seemed to appear out of nowhere.

"No, I'll take the check." Quin said smiling.

"Here you go. Have a great evening." She handed him the check and walked away.

"You don't have to pay. You drove." Trey smiled at him.

"I want to. I haven't had anyone to take care of since my mom passed. Let me do this one little thing."

He paid and they left driving around and talking a little more.

"I have a small apartment. You want to see it?"

"I have work to do in the morning."

"Just for a few minutes." He put his hand on his leg and rubbed it.

"OK, just a few minutes."

They got to his place; it was a small one-bedroom apartment on a second floor. Quin shut and locked the door as soon as they got in. Trey looked weird at him.

"Sorry, just a habit from living in the city so long."

Trey just nodded he understood.

Quin walked up to him put his arms around his waist and pulled him in close. He put his forehead on his and touched noses.

"You are so fucking cute." Quin smiled big.

Trey felt like his knees might give out at any moment.

"I think you are cute as well." Trey barely got out before Quin grabbed his face and kissed him so hard, he had no doubt who was in control.

"I want you. I want you to be my farm boy." Quin said after he released the kiss.

Trey said nothing, just looked at him.

"Come with me my boy." He took Trey's hand and lead him to the bedroom. He took Trey's shirt off and started kissing his chest, working his way down to his waist and back up to his lips. Trey could hardly breathe. He pushed Trey down on the bed and got undressed himself. Got on top of Trey, grabbing the back of his head pushing it toward his chest. Trey wrapped his arms around his chest and pulled him in as he started to kiss his chest. He pushed Trey down and soon he was on his tool.

"Take those pants off." Quin said as he got off of him. Trey did so and Quin kissed him again taking both of them back on the bed. He rolled Trey and took Trey's breath away.

A short time later they were lying in bed Quin holding Trey tight against him.

"I really need to get home." Trey said not really wanting to leave his arms.

"I know. I am just really enjoying having you in my arms."

"I'll come over again."

"Tomorrow?"

"Sure." Trey smiled not believing this hot guy wanted him so much.

The next couple of days they spent dinner together and it always ended up with them in bed.

"Why don't you come over for Thanksgiving?" Trey said to him as Quin was holding him again.

"Really?"

"Yes, I would like that."

"OK, then. What time and what should I bring?"

"Come over in the morning. We will spend the day together. You don't need to bring anything."

"I'll be there."

Trey snuggled back deep into his arms.

"Don't you have to go home?" Quin whispered in his ear as he kissed his neck.

"Not just yet."

Chapter Forty-Five

"Are you OK?" Stan looked at Trey as he paced around the kitchen.

"Listen he is very important to me, please be nice." Trey looked at his brothers who all smiled back. "I shouldn't have invited him."

"It will be fine." Anna gave the others a look.

"We will behave." Eddie said as he sighed.

"Have some faith in us." Clayton patted Trey on the back.

"You must really like this guy." Ruth smiled at him as Sandy chased the little one out of the kitchen again.

"He makes me happy." Trey smiled.

"That's what matters." Ruth said as she finished the potatoes.

"I wish he would get here." Trey sighed and started pacing more.

"Please just go outside and wait for him. You're making me crazy in here." Anna pointed to the door.

Trey went and sat on the front step, looking out the driveway trying to make Quin's car appear.

"You are really taken by this guy?" Ruth sat down beside him.

"I like him a lot." Trey didn't look away from the driveway.

"He treats you good?"

Trey looked at Ruth and smiled. "No worries, I can take care of myself, but yes he does."

"I just don't want to see you get hurt."

"Thank you. I love you."

Ruth put her arm around him and pulled him in close.

"He better get here soon. Dinner is almost ready." She got up and headed in, just as his phone went off.

Trey looked at his phone and he sunk a little.

"What's wrong?" Ruth looked at him.

"He isn't going to make dinner. He will be here later. Something came up."

"Well, at least he messaged you." In truth Ruth didn't believe what she was saying. He waited till almost dinner to message leaving Trey to suffer and she didn't like that at all.

"Well, might as well go in." Trey stood up, his happiness from earlier gone.

"He is coming later. It will be fine." She faked smiled at him again.

Hours later dinner was done and everything was cleaned up. Eddie was having a second piece of pie and a car pulled in.

"He is here." Trey jumped up. "Now please." He looked at his brothers who just shrugged their shoulder's acting all innocent.

Trey half ran out to greet Quin.

"I am so sorry. I have a friend who is bi polar and she was having a meltdown. I was trying to calm her down. She is alone and all."

"You should have brought her with you." Ruth said from the porch as she eyed Quin up.

"She doesn't live around here. I was on the phone. That's why I had to message you instead of calling you."

"It's fine." Trey gave him a big hug.

"I missed you." Quin gave Trey a big hug.

"I missed you to. This is my God Mother, Aunt Ruth." He said as he walked to the porch.

"Pleasure to meet you." Quin stuck out his hand.

"The pleasure is all mine." She shook his hand still eye bawling him.

They made their way passed her and into the house. Ruth sat on the swing; she could hear the introductions. Something in her told her something wasn't right, but she wasn't sure what.

"What's wrong?" Stan asked and startled Ruth.

"What nothing."

"That's not true." Stan sat down beside her.

She looked at him and smiled, patted his leg and went to stand.

"You don't believe him, do you?"

"It's not for me to say."

"Since when?"

She sat back down and looked at him.

"Something about that story doesn't add up to me. He could have just as easily talked to her on the phone here. Second, he was hours late, that's a long time to be on the phone, why not find someone local who could go to her."

"I agree. I don't think Trey sees it though."

"Of course not, he is in love, I mean look at Quin, he is a good-looking guy."

"So, what do we do?"

"Hope for the best, and be ready for his heart to be broke."

"You're not going to say anything?" Stan was a little shocked.

"Oh, honey, you have to know when to keep your mouth shut. Saying something now would look like we don't approve of him being gay, he would withdraw. Then when his heart gets broke, it will make it harder for him to come to us. Sometimes you just have to let life play out."

"I get it. I don't like it, but I get it."

"So, they all sent you out here to get me to step in?"

"I drew the short straw."

She smiled a little at him. "No one wants to stand by and watch a loved one get hurt." She patted him on the knee again and this time got up and headed in. "Now we go pretend we like this guy because we love Trey."

"All those years of community theater will go to good use." Stan stood and smiled.

They walked in and everyone was sitting around the table drinking coffee and chatting. Everyone looked at Ruth waiting for her to step in, but she just poured a coffee and sat down.

Chapter Forty-Six

Trey walked through the Laurel mall not really looking at much. His thoughts were on Quin.

"Are you just going to walk by and not say hi back." Benton playfully hit Trey's shoulder.

"Oh, hey. I was just.."

"In outer space somewhere." Benton laughed.

"Yes, well Quin was supposed to be with me today, but he got called into work."

"Dangers of working in the service industry."

"I guess. His boss is letting us use his cabin for a weekend, so he said he needs to suck up. What are you doing?"

"Trying to get some Christmas shopping done." He held up a couple of bags. "Not finding much."

"That's what I need to do, but I really don't feel like it."

"You're really into Quin, aren't you?"

"I am. I just can't believe someone who looks so good..."

"You're pretty good looking yourself you know."

"Thanks." Trey rolled his eyes.

"Hey, you deserve someone who will treat you good."

"He is very sweet to me. I am very lucky."

"He is very lucky to. Don't forget that."

"I hope he feels that way."

"If he doesn't then he isn't the one for you."

"I think he is definitely the one for me."

"Then I am very happy for you."

"Thank you, don't worry you're still my best friend."

"I better be, and the best man at your wedding."

"Let's not rush things." They both laughed.

"Hey Carl and James are meeting me. Want to hang out with us?"

"Where is Shane?"

"His old job called him; made him an offer he couldn't refuse. He moved back out west."

"Oh, I'm sorry."

"It's all good. He wanted me to go with him, but I have too much here. We weren't really a couple couple anyway."

"Yeah, well uh what did you buy." Trey was trying to get out of this uncomfortable conversation.

"Just a few odds and ends."

"Hey, guys." Carl said as he walked up.

"Did you find anything good?" Benton asked smiling now.

"Not really." Carl shook his head.

"Where did you go." Trey asked.

"We were in Wilkes-Barre shopping."

"I was just heading to Boscov's now." Benton said.

"Yeah, let's go." James smiled.

"You coming with?" Benton looked at Trey.

"No, he should be getting done with work soon, and I got things to do at the farm." He waved as he left.

"He, who?" Carl looked confused at Benton.

"He is seeing that Quin I told you about."

"The one who works at Smokey Bones?" James looked confused.

"Yeah, they called him into work today, so Trey was feeling lonely."

"We had lunch there; we didn't see him at all." Carl's smile left his face.

"Are you sure?"

"Listen we saw pictures of him. We would have seen him if he was there. He wasn't there."

"That's not good." Benton looked in the direction Trey left.

Chapter Forty-Seven

"So, the big weekend is coming up." Ruth said to Trey as he came in from tending the animals.

Ruth had come down to help get the house done for Christmas, everyone was coming and it was only a week away.

"It was supposed to be this weekend, but he canceled again. His job sucks." Trey got a cup of coffee and slumped into a kitchen chair.

"He works a lot." Ruth sat down beside him.

"Well, he has bills with college and all. He said he needs whatever hours he can get."

"I guess I get that." Ruth sipped her coffee.

"At least they are closed for Christmas. He will be here all day."

"Did you get him anything yet?"

"No, I have no idea what to get him."

"It will come to you, I'm sure." Ruth smiled glad he hadn't spent any money on him.

"I was so looking forward to getting away with him for the weekend." Trey said as he stood.

"Where are you off to so fast?"

"I have to go to the feed mill. I need to pick up a few things."

"Do you want me to make something for dinner?"

"You are doing so much already."

"I think your mom is coming with Stan later as well."

"I'll try and make sure I'm home."

Ruth spent the afternoon coming up with a plan in her mind. She didn't like what was going on at all.

"Ruth we are here." Stan said as they walked in.
"Where is my boy?" Anna asked.
"I'm right here mom." Stan said laughing.
"Not you silly." She slapped his arm.
"He went to the feed mill."
"His he ready for his weekend." Anna smiled.
"He canceled." Ruth sighed.
"Again?" Anna was annoyed.
"Yes, work again."
"Something is off here." Stan said anger showing through in his voice.
"I know." Ruth shook her head, as the door opened, they all got quiet.
"Mom, so good to see you." Trey hugged her as he walked into the kitchen.
"Oh, baby. I love you." She kissed him on the cheek.
"So, big weekend?" Stan said pretending not to know anything.
"No. He has to work again."
"Oh, baby. I'm sorry." Anna rubbed his back.
"Dinner is ready." Ruth sat a roast on the table where mash potatoes, corn and bread were already waiting. They all gathered around the table and Ruth said grace.
"Honey, you're not eating." Anna looked over at Trey.
"Yeah, I'm just not very hungry."
They all just looked at each other not sure what to say.
"I found the perfect tree for Christmas eve." Stan said smiling.
"Oh, where?"
"It's on the back field."
"Am I fat?" Trey blurted out.
"What?" Ruth was almost out of her seat.
"No, why would you think that?" Anna asked.
"Is he telling you that?" Ruth was ready to fight now.
"No, not at all. I just…" He put his fork down.

"If he is making you feel that way, that's not cool." Stan tried to look him in the eye.

"I have things to get done at the barn." He stood.

"Aren't you going to finish your dinner." Ruth objected.

"Just not hungry." Trey left waving his hand at the food.

"All this canceling on him is having a bad effect on him." Stan sighed.

"He's not fat." Anna said with a tear in her eye.

"Of course not, that's just ridiculous. Stan, can you pick me up in the morning?"

"Mom and I are actually staying the night."

"Perfect."

The next morning Stan and Ruth left around lunch time.

"So where are we going."

"Smoky Bones. I'm hungry."

"Hungry. I guess it's not for food." Stan smiled.

"You know all those years you spent in community theater?"

"Yes."

"Be ready to put it to use, and follow my lead."

Stan smiled, he didn't know what she had in mind, but he knew she was up to no good.

They walked into Smoky Bones, and were greeted by a man in a tie.

"Oh, you must be the owner. You look so nice in that tie." Ruth said like she wasn't all there.

"Granny no. This is the host. Sorry, she has her good days and her bad." Stan smiled not sure where this was going.

"This isn't the nice guy with the cabin?" She pointed.

"Granny, not the cabin again." He put his arm around her. "Bad day." He whispered to the host.

"So, who is the manager then?" Ruth looked around confused.

"That would be him right there. Tom." The host motioned for an older man, who was also wearing a tie to come over.

"Tom, is that his name? I thought it was Jerry." Ruth kept going on.

"Sorry, to bother you sir. Maybe we should just go." Stan smiled.

"No bother, how are you ma'am?"

"I just wanted to thank you for letting my nephew use your cabin for his honeymoon."

"I'm sorry ma'am. You must be mistaken. I don't own a cabin." The man smiled back.

"Granny I told you this isn't where he works, It's Texas Roadhouse."

"This isn't the Texas Roadhouse?"

"No granny."

"Then why are we here?"

"You said you wanted their wings."

"I don't like wings."

Stan sighed, and looked at the two men standing before him.

"I am so sorry for this. She is having a very bad day."

"It's OK sir." The manager said as he pointed to Ruth who was now heading out the door. Stan smiled and left.

"OK, care to explain that?"

"There never was a cabin. He had told Trey the manager had a cabin he was going to use."

"Very good."

"You did good yourself." She slapped him on his knee, and they backed out and left.

"So, what are you going to do with this information?"

"I'm not sure yet. I just needed to verify that he was lying, He also wasn't working. I watched and no sign of him going in or out of the kitchen."

"So, what do you think all this means?"

"Well on the surface, it looks like he might be two timing him. I think there is more to it though. Time will tell."

Chapter Forty-Eight

"Happy Christmas Eve." Stan said as he and his family walked in.

"Happy Christmas Eve." Ruth said as she heard him enter the kitchen.

"What are you doing?" He looked over her shoulder as she was standing at the stove.

"Making some chicken noodle soup." She smiled at him.

"On Christmas eve?"

"Well, one never knows when you'll need a good cup of soup." She continued to add things to the pot.

"Merry Christmas Eve." Trey said as he entered the kitchen.

"Hey when is Quin getting here?"

"An hour or so."

"Well, mom said that Eddie and Clayton went to cut the tree down already."

"Oh, cool. I love decorating the tree." Trey smiled looked at Ruth. "What are you making?"

"Chicken noodle soup."

"On Christmas Eve?"

"It's chilly out, thought, everyone might like some soup today."

"Boys could you help me with the boxes of decorations?" Anna yelled from the living room.

They both headed into the living room. A short time later Ruth was testing her soup to make sure it was right.

"Shit." Trey came in and flopped down into a chair.

"That language on Christmas Eve?"

"Sorry." Trey just put his head on the table.

"What's wrong?" Ruth knew the answer already.

"Quin isn't coming. He is not feeling good. He wants to stay in bed so he is good for tomorrow." Trey said without lifting his head.

"Well, lucky you." Ruth smiled.

"What?"

"I made chicken noodle soup, what better thing to eat when you're feeling sick."

"Good idea. I'll call him and tell him I'm coming to the rescue."

"Why don't you just surprise him."

"Really?"

"Yes, it would be very romantic. I'll get you some ready." Ruth grabbed the bowl and lid she had set aside.

"But I'll miss the decorating." Trey sighed.

"You don't have to stay long." She handed him the bowl.

"Thank you. You're the best." He grabbed his coat and the bowl and headed out the door.

"How did you know?" Stan said as he came out of the shadows.

"Well, he couldn't use work again, they closed at three today."

"You're good."

"Don't mess with my God child." She pointed the ladle at him.

A short time later Trey was walking up the Quin's apartment door and just as he knocked the door opened.

"OK. I have the presents ready and my bag is packed." Quin said looking back the hall. He turned to see Trey standing there.

"Bags packed, presents?" Trey could feel tears start to come.

"Uh, Trey why are you here?"

"I brought you homemade chicken soup because you said you were sick."

"He bro, I'm going to grab a quick shower before we go." A man said as he walked out the hall way.

"Who is this?" Trey said trying to fight back tears.

"Oh, hey. I'm Wade, Quins brother."

"Brother, right. He doesn't have any brothers."

"Come in." Quin pulled Trey in and closed the door.

"What's really going on here?"

"Quin, who is this?" Wade asked.

"Uh, well."

"I thought I was his boyfriend, but here you are." Trey blurted out.

"I said I'm his brother."

"I can explain." Quin started.

"Tell me you're not up to your old tricks." Wade gave him a dirty look.

"What the hell is going on!" Trey was angry now.

"Quin is a pathological lier." Wade shook his head.

"I am not."

"Quin, please." Wade put his hand up.

"He told me he grew up out west, and his dad was a drunk who his mother left and she passed away a couple years ago from cancer."

"What I meant…"

"You shut up. I want to hear from Wade." Trey put his hand up.

"He is the youngest of six. He has two brothers and three sisters. His dad is a retired state cop, he lives with our mom where we grew up in Juniata County."

"He said he was working to pay his way through college."

"He has a scholar ship. He is very smart."

"What!?" Trey couldn't believe what he was hearing.

"I guess you don't love me anymore, since I have a normal life."

"Wait, so on Thanksgiving when you were late?"

"He was down home, and dipped early." Wade continued. "I thought something was up then."

"You lied?" Trey was still trying to wrap his mind around everything.

"You hate me now." Quin went and sat on the couch.

"I'm sorry man, he never even mentioned you. I would have reached out to you and warned you."

"That's why I didn't tell you, or the family, you always ruin my relationships."

"You ruin them by lying all the time."

"I've been played." Trey was starting to get everything.

"Another relationship down the tubes." Quin put his head in his hands.

"I would have liked you, the real you." Trey said as he turned toward the door.

"So, do you still want to date?" Quin lifted his head and smiled.

"You can't be serious. You need help. I have to get out of here."

"What about my gifts?" Quin asked

Trey spun and looked him in the eyes. "You have ruined my Christmas. My God, you had me thinking I was fat, that you were ashamed to be with me, that was the only reason I could come up with why you canceled on me all the time."

"I'm so sorry he did this to you. We do try and keep tabs on what he does."

"So, you would cancel when your brother was checking up on you?"

Quin just hung his head.

"What about the cabin, did your boss ever say that?"

Quin shook his head no.

"Does he even have a cabin?!"

"I don't think so."

"Oh, my God. You lie about everything."

"I really did want to take you to a cabin."

"I want to do things I can't all the time. I don't lie to people about it."

"I do love you."

"Really, you lie that's how you show love. You're probably lying now. Fuck you! I'm out of here." Trey left slamming the door as hard as he could. He could hear Quin yelling at his brother as he started to walk away. He looked down and realized he didn't have the soup anymore.

"Fuck that." Trey turned and went back in. They both looked confused as he walked in.

"This soup was made with love, from someone who actually loves me. You don't get to enjoy that." He picked up the soup and slammed the door again as he left.

He sat in his car crying uncontrollably for what seemed hours, but was only twenty minutes. He picked up his phone and dialed.

"Hi are you home?"

"Yeah, I'm not going anywhere till the morning."

"Can I come over I really need someone to talk to."

"Sure."

"I'll be there shortly."

He messaged Stan that he wouldn't be home for a while to decorate without him. He really wasn't in the mood anyway.

Chapter Forty-Nine

"Hi, so what's going on?" Benton said as he opened the door.

"Quin, he is a liar." Trey said as he sat at the table.

Benton could see that he had been crying for a while, so he walked over and rubbed his back.

"What happened?" He asked as he sat down beside him.

"He lied about everything. His family, everything."

"What?"

"He is actually the youngest of six, from central pa. Both parents are still very much alive."

"Oh my God, why?"

"His brother said he is a pathological liar. He can't seem to help himself."

"You talked to his brother?"

"He was there when I stopped by to surprise him. I thought it was another guy, I think I would have preferred that."

"I'm so sorry."

"He made me feel sorry for him, no family, no one to turn to for help."

"Sounds like he needs help."

"I'm so broken hearted."

"You have family and friends who love you very much."

"I know."

"They are probably very worried about you right now."

"Why would they be, I haven't told them anything."

"You think she made that chicken soup by accident?"

"Wait how do you know about the soup?"

"I talked to your family the other week, after we ran into you at the mall. I felt something was wrong then."

"Why didn't you say something?"

"Because I wasn't a hundred percent sure, and I didn't want to rain on your parade."

"Still doesn't explain the soup."

"Aunt Ruth called me earlier today. She told me she was making the soup, because she felt like he was going to cancel again."

"She knew and set it up?" Trey was blown away.

"She had a hunch, but she didn't want to say anything."

"Why?"

"Because she was worried that you would take it the wrong way, like they didn't support you. She felt you needed to find out on your own."

"And the soup helped that along."

"Well, it didn't hurt."

"What about the rest of the family?"

"They all thought he was seeing someone else; they have no idea of what you just told me."

"I'm such a fool; how did I not see it." Trey put his head down on the table.

"Love is blind, or rather lust is blind."

"I don't think I am ever going to date again."

"You feel that way now, time heals all."

"You talk to Aunt Ruth too much."

"It's Christmas Eve don't you think you should be with your family?"

"I'm not sure I can go home and face everyone right now."

"They are waiting for you, and worried about you."

"You told them I was coming here didn't you."

"Yes."

"Everyone is talking behind my back."

"Everyone is worried about you. We are just trying to be there for you."

"What do I do?" He looked at Benton his face full of sadness.

"Go home, they are waiting to decorate till you get there."

"What do I say?"

"Tell them everything, tell them nothing. Whatever you feel is right."

"Come with me."

"Well, Aunt Ruth and your mom already asked me to follow you there."

"OK then let's go."

"Just don't tell my Aunt Alice, she wanted me to come there. I told her I would be at Carl's house tomorrow."

"You're a good friend, my best friend."

"I love you like a brother Trey; I will always be here for you."

They both stood and hugged, and headed to their cars. They pulled up in front of the house and walked in together.

"Well, about time you get back. Lots of decorating to do." Anna hugged him and kissed him on the cheek.

"Then let's get to it." Trey tried to smile even though he felt broken inside. Soon the music and eggnog had him feeling a little better.

"Ruff night." Anna said as she found him staring out the kitchen window.

"You have no idea." Trey turned and half smiled.

"When you're ready to talk, I am here for you."

"Thank you."

"I'm sorry he hurt you."

"Me to. I just want to try and put it behind me and enjoy the holiday as much as I can."

"Just remember what the holiday is about."

"What?"

"Jesus was born, and no one loves you more than he does."

Trey smiled at his mother. "You have a good point their mom." Trey went and grabbed his coat.

"Where are you going?"

"I got somethings to do at the barn." He put his coat on and walked down to the barn. He walked in and looked around at the animals as they all seemed to have found a warm place to sleep for the night. Then it occurred to him, that Jesus was born in a place much like this. He looked out the barn door toward the sky. He was hoping to see the north star, but it was cloudy. He looked back at the animals and to a small pile to hay laying near a corner. He walked over and got on his knees.

"Dear God, I know I haven't been the best kind of person, and I don't pray like I should. I know I have no right to ask for help, but I am. I need help getting through this, my heart is broken again, all I really want is someone to love me. I know I have my family and friends, and I am grateful for that, but I need that special someone in my life. I am very grateful for all you have done for me, and please continue to watch over and bless my family and friends. In Jesus name amen." He went to stand up, then went back down on his knees. "Please let Quin get the help he needs. In Jesus name amen." He stood and brushed his knees off.

"Amen." He heard from behind him.

"Aunt Ruth." He said as he looked up.

"That was beautiful. I am so proud of you. You are stronger than you think."

"Thank you. I don't feel that way right now."

"That prayer says otherwise. You prayed for someone who hurt you. That says more about you than you will ever know."

"I don't know about that."

"The bible tells us to love thine enemies."

"Thank you." Trey wasn't sure what to say to that.

She hugged him and they headed back to the house, as they left the barn, Trey looked up, the clouds had cleared and he saw the north star. A smile came across his face, and he felt all warm inside. Ruth could feel a shift in him.

"That's God answering your prayers."

Chapter Fifty

"Thanks for having me over." Benton said as he and Trey hugged.

"You're more than welcome to come tomorrow for Christmas."

"You're trying to get me killed on a holiday." Benton laughed.

"Thank you for everything."

"I told you. You're like a brother. I love you."

"I love you to.""

Trey watched as Benton got in his car and left. He then headed back into the house.

"Well, mom I am very tired." She was finishing her coffee standing by the sink and he walked over and hugged her.

"Are you OK?"

"I'm better than I was earlier. I'll be better tomorrow."

"He just wasn't the right one for you."

"I know."

"The right one will come along."

"I know mom. I'm good."

"It's just that...."

"Don't worry mom, I am fine."

"But that's my job, to worry."

"And you're a great mom." He hugged her again. "Now I have to get to bed or Santa won't stop here."

She laughed and playfully slapped his shoulder.

Trey lay in bed his mind racing. He really wasn't as tired as he had said. He was just tired of everyone looking at him waiting for him to break down. His thoughts drifted through the day, how up and down he had been all day. Although he didn't feel really tired it wasn't long before he couldn't keep his eyes open any longer.

"There you are Trey, took you long enough. Hand me the screw driver. This baler is jammed again."

Trey looked around and he was in the barn, and it was summer. He was totally confused.

"The screw driver."

He looked down and the screw driver was laying where it had always laid. He picked it up and handed it to the out stretched hand.

"Dad?" It finally sank in who had been talking to him.

He pulled his head out of the baler and grabbed the screw driver.

"Who were you expecting, Milton Berle?"

"Not with the old actors again." Trey laughed.

"They were the best times."

Trey looked around still confused as to what was going on.

"I've been waiting for you to come since you went to bed. Took forever for you to fall asleep." He wiped his hand with an old rag.

"Am I dead?" Trey got very concerned.

"This generation, always so dramatic. No, you're not dead."

"Then what is it?"

"I can see you are struggling a little bit."

"A lot right now."

"So, I came to help."

"By bringing me to the barn to fix the bailer?"

"You know you and me, we had our best conversations over this hunk of junk."

Trey smiled a little. "Yes, I guess we did."

"I enjoyed that. I knew we would always get it fixed, and in the process, I got to know you better."

"I guess so."

"That's why I never got rid of it. I never got to do that with your brothers, but you, you were just like me. With the farming anyway."

"I'm trying to make you proud."

"You're doing a heck of a job."

"So, what is it you came to talk to me about?"

"Love will come when it is meant to. You can't rush things, or force it like you were with Quack."

"Quin."

"Whatever. Did I ever tell you about how I met your mother."

"No."

"I was actually after her cousin. She was very good looking, not that your mother wasn't. Her cousin Beth, no wait Betty I believe, aw names aren't important. Anyway, all the guy were after her, rumor was she was easy."

"You dog."

"Yeah, well your old dad here wasn't the football star, not even close, so she over looked me. I tried to force something to happen there, and got my heart broke. I thought I would never fall in love again."

"So, what happen?"

"Two weeks later I was at scoops with my buddies and your mother was walking over, not paying attention, she tripped and fell. She banges up her knee pretty good, cut the palm of her hand. She was crying and while everyone else laughed. I went over and helped her up. I knew a little first aid from health class so I helped her get cleaned up with the first aid kit, then made sure she made it home."

"And you two lived happily ever after."

"No, I was just being nice. I wasn't into her at all."

"OK"

"But she baked some cookies, and brought them to the house as a thank you. We started talking and hanging out as friends. We bonded over the fact that neither of us were A list kids."

"That's sweet."

"My point is I wasn't looking for love, but it found me. It took time, but all good things do. Enjoy the moment you're in and love will find its way to you."

"Thank you, dad."

"You're welcome, now where did I put that screw driver?"

Trey went to pick it up but suddenly he was opening his eyes and he was in his room again. He smiled rolled over and pulled the blanket in close to him.

Chapter Fifty-One

"Hey Aunt Ruth, it's cold out here, why are you sitting on the front porch?" Trey asked as he said down beside her.

"Just thinking." She smiled warmly at him.

"Are you OK?"

"Yes, just missing my kids and my grandchildren."

"Why didn't you go to Colorado with them?"

"Oh, I would have been in the way."

"I don't believe that."

"They were going skiing and God knows what else. They didn't need to worry about me being there to slow them down."

"I can't imagine you slowing anyone down."

"You're so sweet." She patted him on his leg. "But even the drive here is a lot for me anymore. Getting old isn't so much fun."

"I guess not."

"It was nice spending Christmas here with all of you, and I did that live thing this morning and saw my grandchildren open their presents."

"You have Facebook live?"

"Well, your brother had to help me with it, but it was like I was there."

"I love Christmas, but I'm also glad it's over."

"Are you OK?"

"You know I wasn't sure if I would be. I really liked him a lot."

"There will be another."

"I know."

"Who is that?" Ruth looked as a car pulled in.

"I don't believe it."

A lady got out of the car and retrieved at tray of cookies. She walked stone face toward the porch.

"Hi, how are you?" Trey asked confused. Ruth stood behind him even more confused.

"Hi, Trey."

"To what do we owe this visit?"

"Well, your mother and I always trade Christmas cookies. Usually at church, but since I don't go to that church anymore."

"I see." Trey looked passed her to the car.

"So much has changed this year, I just would like to keep one tradition alive." She sighed and noticed where Trey was looking. "Daren didn't come along. He wanted to stay home."

"Oh, how is he?"

"Gale it is so nice to see you." Anna came out with a big smile on her face.

"Well, what kind of Christmas could you be having without my cookies?" Gale finally broke her stone face with a smile as she walked by Trey.

"Who is Daren?" Ruth asked as they both watched the ladies go into the house laughing.

"Her son." Trey sighed.

"I take it you liked him a lot."

"And he liked me, but she forbids it."

"So, that's who you truly love."

"I'm not sure anymore."

"Your face told a different story, when you were looking to see if he was in the car."

"Do you have a couch?"

"What?" Ruth was confused.

"If you're going to be my therapist, I at least want to lay down while we talk."

"Oh, honey you couldn't afford me." Ruth patted him on the shoulder and went inside. Trey followed. His mother was making a tray of cookies for Gale and they were sipping coffee, and getting caught up on things. He walked into the living room where his family all looked at him with concern on their faces.

"What?" Trey held up his hands.

"Are you OK?" Stand asked as he packed up the last few presents to take home.

"I'm fine. I've been over Daren for a while now."

No one believed him and he could see that in their faces.

"Well, it's been a long day, and I think I am tired." Trey turned to head upstairs.

"Sorry, you had such a ruff Christmas this year?" Eddie said.

"Everyone can stop feeling sorry for me. I'm fine." Trey tried to keep himself calm as he spoke, when inside all he wanted to do was scream.

He went upstairs hearing his mother and Gale laughing in the kitchen. He got into bed and laid there taking deep breaths as tears came. He hadn't thought about Daren in a while. He really did miss him, and felt that he could have been the one.

"She is down there laughing and enjoying life, while keeping her son from enjoying his. How could any mother do that?" Trey mumbled to himself as he cried himself to sleep.

Chapter Fifty-Two

Anna watched her baby boy walk up the stairs without saying good night. Gale was going on about the ladies at her new church and noticed her stair.

"How is he doing?" Gale half smiled and sat her coffee down.

"He is heart broke again."

"He is such a nice boy."

"I worry about him. He so wants someone to love."

"I know." Gale picked up her coffee and sipped it.

"And what about Daren?" Anna raised her eyebrow.

"He doesn't talk to me much. He is working for a dairy farmer."

"Does he like it?"

"I couldn't tell you. He goes to work and comes home, that's it."

"Doesn't that bother you?"

"Very much, especially because I know the reason."

Anna knew the answer, but she wanted her to say it. So, she just sat her coffee down and looked at her.

"I know what you're going to say."

"Really, you've become a mind reader."

Gale smiled slightly. "I worry about him. I don't want to see him go; well, you know where."

"I worry about that all the time, but I also know that God is loving and forgiving and doesn't make mistakes."

"I never said he was a mistake."

"I know, I know you love him dearly."

"You have other boys who will make you a grandmother. I don't, he is all I have."

"He can always adopt."

"I know it seems like it should be easy. I should want him to be happy."

"You know eventually he will have had enough and leave you, then you lose him for good."

"I don't want that."

"What do you want."

She looked down at the empty dessert plate in front of her. "My cake and eat it to."

"We both know that's not real world."

"Being a mother shouldn't be this hard."

"You lost one boy, don't lose a second."

"So, I just pretend I'm OK with it?"

"Listen do you want him to think about you and your husband having sex?"

"What? Oh my God no."

"Let me tell you straight or gay your children don't want you thinking about them having sex either."

"So, what do I do?"

"Treat them with the same respect that they give you. If he is with a jerk, treat him that way, if he is with a nice young man, treat him that way." She looked upstairs as she finished.

"He is so sad right now." Gale hung her head.

"You don't want that for your son."

"I don't."

"Then do the right thing."

"Come with me for a minute." Gale stood, and grabbed the plate of cookies Anna had made for her.

"Are you leaving?"

"In a few minutes, it's getting late, but first I want to give you something I have in the car."

Anna was confused, but followed her out the door to the car. She opened the passenger's door, and on the seat sat a neatly wrapped present.

"I didn't get you anything." Anna said looking confused.

"No, read the tag."

She looked and the tag read to Trey, from Daren.

"He sent a present." Anna's face lit up.

"He gave this to me as I was leaving."

"And."

"All he said was please make sure he gets this. I gave him a look and he walked away."

"Why didn't you bring it in when you first got here?" Anna looked confused.

"Well, my first thought was to throw it out at the gas station, but I wouldn't have answers as to how he liked it."

"I see." Anna took a step back.

"Then I figured I would just take it home and say he refused to take it."

"Now?"

"Now, I want him to have it." She picked it up and handed it to Anna.

"Do you know what it is?" Anna asked as she took it.

"No idea." Gale hung her head.

"It's not all bad."

"He needs to be happy I know. I need to but out."

"It could be worse; I mean at least the in laws are great people." Anna smiled at her.

Gale looked up with a little smile on her face. "Do you know my husband would always say thank God we had all boys and you had all boys, that way our families would never be in-laws."

"So, then this is all his fault."

"That's a good way to look at it." Both ladies laughed.

"I'm so glad you came over."

"I needed to talk to you. I wanted you to know I was only doing what I thought was best for my boy."

"I know."

"All I did was make him miserable."

"So now we work to fix that."

"In laws." She laughed again.

"Not to worry they are both rolling over in their graves." Anna assured her.

"I have got to get going. It is late."

They hugged quickly and Anna watched her leave, knowing she just did the hardest thing any mother can do. Admit she was wrong. She smiled at that thought.

"God forbid the day ever comes I have to do that." She laughed and went back inside.

Chapter Fifty-Three

"Good morning." Trey said as he walked into the kitchen. He stopped as he started to pour his coffee feeling like he was being staired at. He looked back to see his mom, Ruth, Eddie and Clayton all looking at him in a weird way. Stan and his family had left the night before, or they would be looking at him to he figured. He just wasn't sure why.

"Good morning honey." Anna smiled at him.

"What's going on?" Trey wasn't really in the mood for whatever weird thing his family was about to unload on him.

"Nothing really." Eddie kind of threw his hands in the air.

"Yeah, I'm going back to bed." Trey sat his coffee back on the counter.

"Now, just get your coffee and have a seat here beside me." Anna smiled at him.

"I'm going to regret this, I am sure." Trey muttered to himself. He took his coffee and grabbed the chair and pulled it out. "What's this?" He looked at the small present sitting on the chair.

"Why don't you pick it up and find out." Ruth smiled at him.

He sat his coffee on the table, picked up the present and sat down. He looked around the table, and they all had goofy smiles.

"What is going on?" Trey narrowed his eyes and looked at them.

"Nothing." Clayton smiled.

"Read the tag." Ruth pointed.

"To Trey From." Trey stopped and looked around at everyone.

"From who?" Eddie asked.

"Are you guys messing with me?"

"OK your brothers maybe, but honey Aunt Ruth and I would never." Anna said.

"Hey!" Eddie and Clayton both yelled.

"But how?"

"He sent it with his mother last night. Gale and I had a long talk." Anna patted his shoulder.

"Open it honey." Ruth urged him.

Trey slowly opened the box. He pulled tissue paper out and looked inside.

"What is it. We have all been trying to guess." Eddie blurted out.

Trey pulled out a hand made wooden picture frame. There was a yellow sticky note covering the five by seven picture. It read I really miss you.

"What's the picture." Ruth asked.

Trey pulled off the note. It was a selfie that Daren had taken of the two of them at the restaurant when they went on that double date. In graved at the bottom of the frame was. First Date 10/15/24.

"When was that?" Ruth asked.

"He had set up a double date, that was awful."

"Looked like you two had a good time." Anna said.

"That was before the girls got there. He put his arm around me and insisted on taking this picture."

"What are you going to do?" Clayton asked.

"I don't know."

"Do you miss him?" Anna asked.

"Yes."

"Then go see him." Anna continued.

"But his mother…"

"She will be fine."

"This is a lot right now. I think I just want to go get the barn work done." Trey took the picture and went to his room. He set it on his night stand and smiled at it. "I miss you to." He smiled at the picture and went back down stairs.

"Aunt Ruth are you leaving?"

"Honey I was planning on being on the road already, but I wanted to know what was in the box. I'm old I have to live through you now." She smiled at him.

"Where are your bags?"

"Your brothers have already put them in the car."

"I miss you when you're not here."

"Honey, I miss you to. I don't know how many more times I'll be up. I'm getting old and this trip, however short is a lot on this old body."

"I will do my best to come see you." Trey said as he walked her to her car.

"I know you will." She smiled knowing he wouldn't.

Just as she went to get into her car another car neither of them knew pulled in. It took Trey a minute to realize who it was.

"No way, what is he doing here?"

"Who is it my dear?"

"Wade, Quin's brother."

"I would love to stay and see what it is about, but I must be getting on the road."

"Thank you, Aunt Ruth I can handle this."

Aunt Ruth backed out as his mother and brothers appeared on the porch. Wade got out of his car and sheepishly walked toward Trey.

"What is it you want?" Trey asked.

By his tone, his brothers knew this wasn't a good visit and started off the porch.

"I got this." Trey held up his hand for them to stay back.

"I just really want to talk to you." He looked over Trey's shoulder. "Alone."

"I'm not sure we have much to talk about."

"You're right we probably don't. I'll just take a few moments of your time."

"Walk with me to the barn. I have work to do you can talk to me while I work."

He followed Trey to the barn.

"First I want to tell you how sorry I am."

"You didn't do anything."

"I know, but I hate when Quin does this. He sees a professional you know."

"I did not know that. Wait I didn't know anything about the real Quin." Trey said as he started feeding the chickens.

"I really do believe he loves you."

"What do you want me to do with that?" Trey stopped and looked back at him.

"Listen he has always let me know about who he is dating. He can't keep a secret, but with you he did."

"So."

"That means to him you are special."

"That's nice, but I can't live with someone I can't trust. Someone I never know if he is lying or not."

"I understand that."

"Then I guess there is nothing else to talk about."

"Well." He scratched his head a little.

"What?"

"He sent a present for you."

"I don't want it."

"I tried to tell him that. He really wanted to come, but I talked him out of it."

"Good. I don't wish him any harm. I hope he gets the help he needs, but I don't want anything to do with him."

"I understand."

"What?" Trey could tell there was something else on his mind.

"So, I take it you're not seeing anyone."

"That's really none of your business."

"Well, I was hoping that maybe." He cocked his head a little at looked at Trey

"What?"

"Well, I've been looking for someone for a while now."

"You know I slept with Quin, your brother, wouldn't you find it weird to sleep with me."

"No, that wouldn't bother me."

"Really?"

"I mean, it's hard to find a guy who is so kind and caring. With running my own business, I don't have a lot of free time. I have been looking for a long time, I could take very good care of you."

"Your whole family is nuts." Trey threw his arms in the air and walked away.

"You won't even give me a chance."

"Not, only no, but hell no." Trey turned and walked toward him.

"Quin said he fell in love with you at first sight and I can see why."

"Do you hear yourself?"

"He also said you like being a good boy, that's what I need in my life."

"I don't want to be your boy."

"I like your spirit."

"I don't know who has the bigger problem, you or your brother."

"Listen I get what I want, and what I want is you."

"I can't believe what I am hearing. I think you need to go, and don't come back."

"Are you sure?"

"Never more." Trey was in his face now.

"OK, if you change your mind this is my number." Wade took his business card wrapped in a hundred-dollar bill, grabbed Trey by his belt, pulling him forward and shoved it down the front of his pants.

"You can play hard to get all you want, but I always win in the end." Wade whispered in his hear and let him go.

Wade turned and walked out of the barn leaving Trey standing confused. On one hand he like being handled like that, on the other that whole family must be nuts, and then there was always Daren to consider.

Chapter Fifty-Four

Trey walked into the kitchen and his mother and Eddie were having coffee.

"So, what was that this morning?" Eddie asked as Trey got a cup of coffee.

"That was Quin's brother Wade."

"What on earth did he want?" Anna looked over at him.

"Well, he started off by saying how much Quin loved me, and that he had a present in the car from him."

"What did you say."

"I told him I didn't care and that I didn't want the present."

"Good for you." Anna sipper her coffee.

"Then he suggested we get together." Trey said as he cut himself a piece of cake.

"What?" Eddie almost yelled, as Anna spit her coffee out.

"You heard me." Trey grabbed his cake and coffee and headed to the table, where Anna was now cleaning up her coffee.

"That is unbelievable." Anna put the cloth back in the sink.

"There is more." Trey reached into the front of his pants, as Anna and Eddie looked confused. He threw the money and business card on the table.

"What's this and why was it in your pants like that?" Anna asked.

"That's where he shoved it, as he whispered in my ear that he always gets what he wants."

"Oh my, he has a lot of nerve."

"Shit." Eddie said as he looked at the business card.

"What?" Trey looked at him.
"Do you know who this is?"
"No."
"He is the guy who has been buying up land around here and building houses and selling them. He is making a fortune. I mean he has several developments."
"So."
"One guess as to who bought Daren's farm."
"Are you serious?"
"Yes."
"That." Trey didn't finish his sentence because his mother was sitting there. He grabbed the money and card.
"Where are you going?" His mother asked as he headed in a huff toward the door.
"To visit Wade." He left the screen door slam behind him as Eddie and Anna staired at each other.

A few minutes later Trey pulled into what used to be the drive way of Daren's farm. The barn was gone as well as the old farm house. In its place a new house was being built, as were two others in what used to be a hay field. Trey got out of the truck, men were working, a few gave him a look, but most just kept on working.

"That was quicker than I expected. I must be getting better." Wade said as he walked toward him.
"Why didn't you tell me?"
"That I bought this place, That I knew who you were a long time ago?"
Trey took his hand and slapped the money and card into it.
"You know I love Daren."
"Well, not that much you dated my brother."
"You know why I can't see Daren."
"Yes, his mom. Not a very nice lady."
"How long did you know your brother was seeing me?"

"Now that I had no idea. When you walked in that day, I knew who you were."

"But you said nothing."

"I wanted to see how it would play out."

"You wanted to see if you could swoop in."

"I can't help it if I love a country boy."

"So, you think I'm just going to jump at you because you have money?"

"Listen, I can take you away from all that farm work. You could stay home, take care of the house and me. Have anything you want."

"I enjoy farm work. I'm not a house wife."

"I bet you would make a good house wife, or boy" He touched Trey's cheek lightly. Trey slapped his hand.

"There's that spirit, I'm going to enjoy breaking it."

"You have me all wrong."

"I could buy your farm…"

"Stop right there, it's not for sale and neither am I."

"Then why are you here?"

"To give your money back."

"You did that, and yet you're still standing there."

Trey wanted desperately to go, to jump in his truck and throw dirt, but he couldn't move. His stomach was in knots. Tear started coming to his eyes and anger built in him. Some of the anger was toward Wade, and some at himself.

"Nothing to say. Good first lesson. Don't talk back." Wade smiled at him.

"I don't need any lessons from you."

Wade grabbed his jaw with his hand and pulled him in.

"I will teach you a lot boy."

"You wish." Trey went to pull away and was surprised at how strong Wade was.

"You go ahead and go, you'll be back."

"I don't think so." He finally pulled his face away.

Wade grabbed him by his pants again and pulled him in close, and whispered in his ear. "Like I said I always get what I want." He let him go just enough that they were face to face looking directly into each other's eyes. The passion and determination Trey saw there made him weak in the knees and he hated himself. Wade reached up with his free hand grabbed a hand full of hair on the back of his head and pulled him in and kissed him like he owned him. Trey pushed him off.

"I'm going now." Trey climbed into his truck.

"You'll be back." Wade yelled as he pealed out of the drive.

Chapter Fifty-Five

"I understand honey, please tell the kids we said hi…. Yes, love you." Anna hung up her phone.

"Who was that?" Trey asked as he hung more New Year's Eve decorations.

"That was Ruth, her kids came home early, they missed her. So, she isn't coming for the party."

"I'm happy for her, I know she missed them. I will miss her."

"Me to. She is a sweet old dear, don't know how many more years we have left with her."

"So, what do you think?" Trey stood back and looked at his handy work.

"Looks great." She looked at him and his mind was nowhere near his body.

"I could use some eggnog." Trey smiled slightly.

"Did you hear anything from him?"

"No. I sent the message days ago." He sighed and poured the eggnog.

"Hey everyone." Chris's voice came as he entered.

"Your back. We missed you so much." Anna ran and hugged him.

"I know, I really wanted to spend Christmas with you guys, but my deposit was not refundable."

"I know dear how was it?"

"Everything I was hoping for and more. An Alaskan cruise over Christmas. The food was so good and always available, and the ship was decorated so beautiful."

"So glad you had a good time." Anna smiled.

"Coffee." Trey held up the pot.

"Yes." Chris looked around. "Are we having a New Year's Eve party?"

"Why yes we are." Trey smiled as he poured his coffee.

"I'm not interrupting anything?"

"Don't be stupid, your family. I just didn't know if you would be back in time."

"So, who is he?" Chris narrowed his eyes and looked at Trey.

"What makes you think that."

"You're shaking as you pour the coffee and you're hosting a party. That's not like you. Even in the short time I have spent with you I know that."

Anna laughed and Trey gave a dirty look.

"Daren sent him a gift at Christmas so he is throwing a party and invited him."

"Really? What about his mother?"

"That is who delivered the gift. We had a long talk." Anna smiled.

"Maybe I should let the two of you talk. I have to go take a shower." Trey groaned a little, knowing they would be talking about him.

A short time later he came back down dress in his best jean, boots and flannel shirt. Extra old spice on, he was hoping he hadn't over done it. The house was filling up with people. His brothers were there as well as Stan's wife and little one. Carl, James, and their crew were there, and his Aunt must have cooked up a storm, because the amount food had doubled in size now.

"Hey buddy, thanks for the invite. It's nice to go to someone else's place for a change." Carl said as he gave him a hug.

"You're more than welcome."

"You smell great."

"I didn't overdo it."

"Not at all."

"Hey everyone." Benton's voice came from the front door.

"More food." Trey just looked as he carried in a crock pot.

"Never come empty handed." Benton smiled at him.

Trey followed him to the kitchen and showed him where to sit the crock pot. Benton turned and hugged him.

"Ok who is he?"

"What?" Trey tried not to smile.

"You're throwing a party, dressed like you're going to church and smell great. Who is he?"

"I really need to start being more unpredictable." Trey half smiled.

"So."

"Daren is supposed to be coming."

"What about his mother?"

"Well, I invited her to."

"So, she gave you her blessing then?"

"Well, I wouldn't say blessing, but she is coming around."

Eddie got the music going and people filed in and out of the kitchen and living room eating, drinking and dancing. Trey tried to have fun, but as time passed, he felt less like partying. His heart was sinking, he was sure his mother was not letting him come. He was soon just sitting on the front porch step.

"Here you are?" Alice sat down beside him.

"Hey." Trey looked up and smiled at her.

"You know a good host would be making sure all his guest were having fun." She smiled at him.

"I know I'm sorry."

"Are you OK?" She sat down beside him.

"I guess."

"I wouldn't be if I were you." She shook her head.

"Excuse me?" Trey looked at her.

"Well, you just had your heart broke from a guy who lied to you about his whole life, his brother then hit on you. The love of your life sends you a gift, and now looks like he may be standing you up. That's a lot."

"Is there something wrong with me?"

"Oh honey, yes." She patted him on the back.

"What?" Trey was shocked at her answer.

"You question your self-worth all the time. You let how people treat you determine how you feel about yourself. It's their loss if they don't want you. Start loving yourself, then someone else can love you."

Trey looked at her confused. "You sound like my mother."

"Well mother's know best. Now how about you come in and be a good host."

They stood and turned to go in and a car pulled in.

"Is that him?"

"Yes." Trey smiled so hard it hurt his face.

He walked off the steps slowly as Daren and his mother got out of the car.

"Are we the last to arrive?" Gale asked as she carried a crock pot.

"Yes."

"Your message said it started at nine." Daren said as he shut his car door. "It's only nine ten."

"It started at six." Trey looked confused.

"Thanks for the invite." Gale smiled at him as she walked by him heading to the kitchen with yet more food.

Daren pulled out his phone. "See it says nine."

Trey looked at his phone and shook his head. "I was nervous when I was sending it."

"Nervous, why?"

"I was worried you wouldn't come."

"I wouldn't miss it." They stood and staired at each other for what seemed forever.

"Well, hug, kiss or something already." Alice's voice came from behind them.

Trey looked over his shoulder and Daren lowered his head and laughed a little. Alice was still on the porch and everyone else was either at the door or looking out the windows.

"Some privacy would be nice." Trey yelled at the house.

"Well, I see he shows up and we are all nobody's now." Alice laughed as Anna held the door open for her. Slowly the faces in the windows disappeared as Anna was yelling at them.

"I've missed you." Trey said slowly and he reached for Daren's hands.

"I've missed you more." Daren grabbed his arms and pulled him in tight for a hug. Trey never felt happier in his life. Feeling Daren's arms around him again, he never thought that would happen.

"I'm sorry if I hurt you." Daren said as he let him go. And grabbed his face with both hands. "I should have never listened to my mother."

"I understand." Trey smiled tears in his eyes. Daren pulled his face in and kissed him so softly. It seemed to last forever.

"Um I'm being a bad host." Trey said trying to pull himself together.

"What?"

"Maybe we should go in and join the others." Trey smiled.

"I really want to take you to the barn and just spend time with you, but inside is probably the right thing to do." He kissed him again, and they went in.

The next three hours seemed to fly by. Trey hadn't smiled that much in a long time. His heart felt full. Midnight was close and Daren grabbed his hand and took him to the porch.

"What?"

"I want you to myself at midnight. The best way to start my year."

They heard everyone counting down. Daren pulled Trey in tight as they got to one and Daren grabbing the back of his head kissing him hard not letting go. When he finally let go, they both just looking into each other's eyes, and Trey knew that's where he wanted to be the rest of his life.

Chapter Fifty-Six

Trey woke, looking at his phone and smiled. He sat on the edge of his bed and sent a message.

Love you looking forward to tonight, can't wait to see what you have planned.

A message came back almost immediately.

Love you too. Also looking forward to tonight.

Trey smiled. He hurried through a shower and was soon downstairs having coffee. The house was empty, his brothers were both away with school and work. He loved sitting in the kitchen just looking around and soaking up the quiet. He was soon out at the barn. He was slowly getting more and more animals, and soon would be at the level his father had the farm.

"So big plans tonight?" The guy from the feed mill asked as he dropped off a delivery.

"Yes, I can't wait." Trey smiled. Barry was his name and he was nice enough, but Trey hadn't told him everything about his life. He wasn't sure how he would handle it so he decided to not say anything.

"Women love this holiday; my wallet hates it." He laughed.

"So do you have plans?"

"Shit no, I'm divorced, Happier this way." He smiled at Trey.

"I guess your wallet is happier as well?" Trey laughed.

"Dammed right."

Trey looked at him for a minute and thought that if he were looking, he might try and hook up with him. Then he spit. He chewed Levi Garret, always had a wad in his mouth. Trey looked at the ground where his spit landed and smiled.

"Thank God I'm not looking." Trey said a little louder than he wanted to.

"What's that?" Barry turned back as he went to get into his truck.

"I was saying I'll go get you a check." Trey smiled and walked toward the house.

Barry followed him to the house and waited on the porch.

"Here you go." Trey said as another truck pulled up.

A man got out and walked up to Trey.

"These are for you." He handed him a large metal, country pale filled with all different kinds of flowers in blue and purple.

"Thank you." Trey said pulling a five out of his pocket and handing it to him.

"You know maybe you guys got the right idea." Barry smiled as he spit again.

"Excuse me?" Trey wasn't sure what he meant.

"Well, I mean I'm not gay, don't think so anyway, but you and Daren seem happy, and I never got flowers from my wife."

"How did you…"

"Oh, please you two are the talk of the feed mill. Two gay farmers. The old men that hang out there are running mouths like duck's asses."

"I see, I just never said."

"I know, I have great respect for you. You don't push who you are on anyone. You keep it in the bedroom where it belongs. Or maybe in the barn." Terry laughed.

"Yes, well."

"Please don't tell me if it's the barn. I don't need that mental image." Barry spit again and laughed on his way back to the truck.

Trey watched him leave and turned and walked into the house with the flowers. Sitting them on the table he took the card out and read it.

"Be ready by five, a limo will pick you up. XOXO." He smiled, laying the note on the table and ran upstairs to get ready.

He was downstairs waiting, at five o'clock a long white limo pulled up to the house. Trey walked out as the driver stepped out and opened the back door for him. Trey looked around surprised Daren wasn't there.

"He said he will see you there, sir."

"Really, and where is there?"

"I am not permitted to say." The man smiled at him, and motioned for him to get into the limo.

"Very well." Trey almost bounced into the limo he was so happy.

"Please help yourself to anything in the bar sir." The man said as he closed the door.

Trey looked around and could not believe how decked out this limo was, it couldn't have been cheap. He wasn't sure he liked Daren spending this kind of money on him.

The black tinted window between him and the front of the car came down.

"If you need anything just ask Sir."

"Thank you I'm fine."

"He asked me to take your cell phone. I'll hold it here till the end of the evening. He doesn't want anyone to bother the two of you."

"Um, OK." Trey slowly handed him the phone.

"He has a very special evening planned for the two of you. Sit back and enjoy." The window went up, and Trey sat back and smiled thinking about Daren. After a few minutes he made himself a jack and coke and sipped at it as they drove on.

"OK, baby I'm here." Daren said as he entered the house. "I have reservations at your favorite place."

Daren looked around the house, but Trey was nowhere to be found. He went into the kitchen and saw the flowers and note. He picked up the note and read it. Tears formed in his eyes, and he threw the small bouquet of flowers he had in his hands on the floor.

Chapter Fifty-Sevem

Daren sat at the kitchen table, and tried to call Trey for the third time, and once again it went to voice mail. He put his head on the table as tears filled his eyes.

"I'm stronger than this!" Daren stood and looked at the flowers on the table and with one swipe he sent them flying against the wall and walked out.

"What are you having?" A bar tender asked Daren as short time later as he sat at the bar.

"Coors light, draft please." He laid money on the counter.

"Hey." A voice came from behind him.

"Barry, hey how are you?"

"I'm great no women taking my money this year." He laughed. "Scotch please." He said as the bar tender was already pouring it for him.

"Lucky you." Daren moaned.

"Why are you here?"

"I don't know why."

"After the flowers you sent Trey, I figured you guys had a big night planned."

"They weren't from me."

"Trey seemed to think they were."

"How do you know about the flowers anyway?"

"I was there when they came. Never seen Trey smiled so big."

"Really?"

"Yeah, I said my wife never bought me flowers, and I said I was happy for you guys or something like that."

"What did he say?"

"He was looking forward to whatever you guys were going to be doing. I said I didn't want to know, I didn't need any pictures in my mind."

"Do you know who delivered the flowers?"

"It was just a white panel van, no name or anything on it."

"Shit!"

"What's wrong?"

"I'm not sure, but I don't like what I'm thinking now."

Daren left his beer and ran out the door as he started making calls. Soon he was back at the farm house and Trey's mother was there.

"Sorry for the mess, I was upset and sent the flowers flying." He said as he walked in on her cleaning it up.

"It's OK, something is wrong. Trey loves you and was looking forward to tonight. I don't like this at all."

"Any idea who it could be?"

"No, all the floral places are closed. I don't know of any with a white panel van."

"Someone went through a lot of trouble to make him think I sent him those flowers."

"Yes, but why?"

"I don't know, he doesn't really have any enemies that I know of."

"Maybe someone wants to hurt you?"

"I can't think of anyone that would do this."

"Did you try and call him again."

"Several times, it just goes to voice mail."

"The locator on his phone isn't working either." She shook her head.

"What do we do?"

"I don't know."

"Did you hear something?" She held up a finger and they were both quiet. All they heard was the silence of the night. Daren started pacing frustrated he had nowhere to start. The he came to a dead stop.

"What's wrong?" She asked as he looked to the door.

"That!" He sprinted out the door. She looked over to see an envelope on the floor. She grabbed it and ran out the door. "Did you see anything."

"Tail lights in the distance. I would never be able to catch them." The cold air of the night wrapped around them as they stood there in disbelief.

"How did someone get onto the porch without us hearing them?" She looked at the envelope. The front of the envelope just said Daren.

"It's to you." She handed it to him.

He took it and just looked at it. Part of him wanted to rip it open, and another part was afraid of what was inside.

Chapter Fifty-Eight

"Driver, can you turn down the heat. It's roasting back here."

"I know sir, the thermostat is stuck. Take off your coat we will soon be there."

"We have been of the road for a while. Where are we going?"

"You will see."

It was almost another half hour when the limo pulled into a drive way that led to a large barn. They pulled inside the barn and the door closed behind them as the limo came to a stop.

"He is waiting for you in the room just over there." The driver pointed to a room in the corner of the building.

"Thank you." Trey said looking confused. He had never seen this place before. He got out slowly and the driver shut the door.

"Oh, my coat." Trey turned back to the limo

"It will be fine there. Now go he is waiting."

Trey was still confused at what was happening. Why was Daren being so weird. Trey walked slowly toward the office and the door opened. As the door shut behind him, he could hear the limo start and leave.

"Daren what is going on?"

"You assume too much." A voice came from behind him.

Trey turned and Wade was standing there smiling at him.

"What is going on?"

"You assumed it was Daren who set this up. Not wise to assume."

"I'm leaving." Trey turned toward the door.

"Go ahead I'm not stopping you. It six degrees outside, windchill about five below. You're in the middle of nowhere, almost two hours from home. I mean providing you head in the right direction. You don't know the direction you came though do you. No coat, no phone. Seems like you're stuck here for now."

"What do you want?"

"You, I told you I always get what I want."

"You can't kidnap me and think you will get away with it."

"I did no such thing; I sent you flowers and asked you to come here. You did that willingly. My driver asked for your phone, you gave it to him no problem, and you left your coat in the car. No one took if from you."

"You think you're so smart." Trey was furious at how he had let himself be tricked.

"No need to be mad. We have a lovely dinner here, and the driver will take you home later."

"After Daren is gone, he will have seen the flowers, and think I'm seeing someone else."

"If he assumes things and doesn't trust you maybe he isn't the guy for you."

"And you are?" Trey spun to face him.

"Well, I do have a nice dinner here for us, I mean what did Daren do?"

"One I didn't ask for nor do I want." Trey turned and looked out the window. Snow had started to fall, and the wind picked up.

"You can go if you want." Wade said softly, as he walked up behind Trey.

"You keep saying that, yet you know it's not reality. I can't go. No coat, no phone I'm stuck somewhere I don't know." Trey was trying to hold himself together and not totally loose it.

"Then sit down and eat." Wade put his hands on Trey's shoulders and squeezed gently. Trey brushed him off.

"It's not nice to be rude to your host." This time he grabbed Trey harder and Trey couldn't bush him off.

"Fine I'll sit." Trey said not wanting to get into a fight, he wasn't sure what he was capable of and didn't want to push his luck. Not yet anyway.

"That's a good boy. You'll fine if you're a good boy you and I will get along great." He pulled out the chair and Trey sat down.

For the first time Trey really looked around. He was setting at a small table in the middle of the room. There were candles on the table and to meals covered with silver metal lids, a bottle of wine was chilling. He looked over in the corner was a small bed, by the bed was an electric heater that was doing a good job of keeping this little room warm. A small desk sat on the other side of the room with a radio on it. There was nothing else in the room.

"It's not much, but it's our first date, I don't want to flash all my money right away." Wade smiled and took the lids off the plates to reveal a prime rib dinner, with baked potato and corn.

"Eat, eat," Wade said as he sat down.

They slowly started to eat.

Chapter Fifty-Nine

Daren and Anna sat at the kitchen table as he opened the envelope.
Dear Daren;
I'm sorry to be telling you like this, but I have met someone else. I'm in love with him, and I'm selling the farm and moving in with him, I hope you can move on.
Trey

Daren laid the note down on the table.

"He didn't write that." Anna said flatly.

"I don't think he did either, but I don't understand what's going on."

"He would never sell this farm, after everything he went through to keep it."

"I know. We talked about how we were going to grow it. We need to figure out what's going on though. I'm worried about him."

"Me to. He had to think that those flowers were from you, that's the only reason he would have gone."

"Yes, but I don't have money for a limo, he should know that."

"So, who would want the two of you broke up?"

Daren and Anna looked at each other thinking the same thing.

"She wouldn't go this far? Would she?" Anna asked.

"She is very controlling. If I find out she had anything to do with this I am done with her."

"Listen I just talked to your mother the other day, and she seemed like she was happy for the two of you."

"If not her, then who?"

"I don't know, none of this makes any sense."

Just then a car came up the drive and parked.

"Speak of the devil." Daren said as they both looked out the window.

Gale got out of the car, went to the passenger side of the car getting something out. She then walked to the house.

"Why are you here?" Gale looked confused as Daren met her at the door. "I didn't think you boys would be back yet."

"Why are you here?" Daren returned the question as she walked in.

"I brought you guys a cake I made for you. I was going to just put it on the table for when you got back. Anna you're here to?" Gale said as she sat the cake down.

"A cake?" Daren looked suspicious.

"Yeah." She lifted the lid off the cake plate and there was a heart shaped cake with Daren and Trey's names on it. "It's chocolate fudge cake."

"That's very nice of you." Anna smiled. "Isn't it Daren?"

"What's going on here? Where is Trey?" Gale kept looking back and forth at them.

"We don't know." Anna sighed.

"What? Why?"

"Someone sent him flowers, then a limo to pick him up. We think he thought it was me, but it wasn't. Now he isn't answering his phone and we have no idea where he is." Daren handed her the note.

"That was slid under the door when we were in the kitchen." Anna told her.

Gale read the note and looked at the two of them. "You don't think that I had anything to do with this?"

They were both quiet.

"Listen I know I wasn't for this in the beginning, but I'm fine now." Gale looked at them. "I even made your favorite cake."

"Mom, I love you."

"Honey, I love you to. I told you that I have never seen you so happy. That I was sorry for everything." Gale was almost in tears.

"I know mom. I just don't understand what is going on."

"I will help figure it out."

"Sorry, Gale. You just seemed like the most logical choice."

"It's not me. I have even been telling my friends how happy I am for them. Just last week I saw that nice man who bought the farm at the grocery store. He asked how you were doing and I told him."

"Oh, Gale we are just going crazy..."

"You saw who at the store?" Daren interrupted.

"You know that nice man that bought our farm."

"And what did you say to him?"

"He asked how you were doing. I told him that you and Trey were seeing each other, that you had big plans for prime rib dinner for valentines. That's all."

"Oh my God!" Daren slapped the table.

"Wade, how did we not think of him?" Anna threw her hands in the air.

"Am I missing something?"

"The nice man's name is Wade, and he has been after Trey. He told Trey he always gets what he wants." Anna updated Gale.

"Oh, I swear I didn't know that."

"I know mom, we figured he had given up. That happened toward the end of last year." Daren said as he scrolled on his phone.

"What are you doing?" Anna asked.

"I think I still have a number for him somewhere in my phone. Yep, there it is."

They all waited as the phone rang and rang.

Chapter sixty

"Hello."

"He answered." Daren said with his hand over the phone. The two ladies pushed him and motioned for him to talk.

"Where is Trey? I know he is with you."

"I'm here Daren, I'm OK." Trey said in the back ground.

"Where are you, I'll come get you."

"No need to do that. I'll be home in the morning."

"He is fine. I will take very good care of him."

"Trey, please I want to spend this night with you." Daren sounded hurt.

"I know, but Wade went through a lot of trouble. We will do something another time."

"I thought you loved me."

"I do."

"I think maybe he needs time to figure out who he is in love with." Wade jumped in.

"Listen here Wade."

"Listen we have to go now. I'll call you tomorrow and we can talk." Trey said and the line went dead.

"AI is great." The limo driver said as he laid down the phone and smiled.

Inside the small room of the building Wade looked at his smart watch and saw a message from the driver. He knew all had gone well.

"Why are you not eating my love." Wade smiled at him.

"I hate you." Trey glared at him.

"After all the trouble I went through for you tonight?"

"I didn't ask for this."

"But I want to take care of you."

"I don't need taken care of." Trey pushed himself away from the table and started pacing again.

"I will be good to you. You will never want for anything."

"If I want something I will earn it. I don't need anyone to give it to me." Trey stopped and looked out the window.

"It's too cold for you to go anywhere." Wade walked up behind him and started to rub his shoulders.

"Please don't touch me."

"I just wanted to make you feel better."

"Then take me home." Trey spun and looked into his eyes.

"I'm not sending my driver out in this weather tonight."

Trey turned and walked away before he hit him. His anger was building up to the point where he wasn't sure he could control himself anymore.

"You should give me a chance. I'm a nice guy."

"Nice guy! You took me away from my boyfriend on Valentine's Day."

"I didn't take you; you came of your own free will."

"You tricked me."

"I want to show you what you could have."

"A bed and table in a corner room, that's great!" Trey threw his hands in the air.

"I mean me." Wade walked over and pushed Trey down on the bed and sat beside him.

"Do you really think this is the way to get someone to want to be with you?"

"Well, I tried talking to you, but you wouldn't give me the time of day."

"That's because I'm not interested."

"Just give me a chance." He reached over grabbed Trey's head and pulled him close and kissed him on the neck.

"What the hell are you doing?" Trey pushed off and was standing once again.

"I want you."

"I want to go home."

"You want to go home?" Wade sounded a little annoyed now.

"Yes."

"Then amuse me."

"Amuse you!"

He sat back down on the bed and patted the bed for him to sit beside him.

"You are joking, right." Trey almost laughed at him.

"No. If I can't have you, I want at least one time with you, so you know what you are missing."

"So, you can have something to cause me more problem. I have a boyfriend who I love. What don't you understand about that?"

"Listen to me boy. I will have you." Wade walked over to Trey and grabbed him under the chin, Trey was surprised again at his strength. He thought to hit him, but controlled himself, and just pushed off.

"Listen you can't force me, that's rape." Trey said as he took several steps back.

"Who is going to believe you over me? You came here willingly for a Valentine's Day dinner, where there is a bed."

"Just take me home please."

"You're more than welcome to leave, walk where ever you want to." Wade smiled at him.

Trey thought to beat him up, but that would only lead to legal problems and he didn't want to lose the farm. Not to this guy. No one knew where he was so help wasn't coming. He looked over and Wade was sitting back on the bed smiling at him. He wanted to cry; he was so mad. He slowly walked over to the bed.

"That's a good boy."

Chapter Sixty-One

"That wasn't Trey." Anna shook her head after Daren hung up.

"I know it wasn't." Daren was doing something on his phone.

"How do you know?" Gale asked.

"He would have asked me to take care of the animals in the morning."

"That is true." Anna nodded in agreement.

"But it sounded just like him?" Gale looked confused.

"He used AI." Daren smiled at them.

"What are you doing?" Anna looked at him as he smiled.

"I put this app on the phone a while back. Mom has a habit of getting lost then calling not knowing where she is. This app will tell me."

"So, you know where he is?" They both were excited.

"Yep, outside a place called Richfield. It's about two hours away on a good day."

"The snow is coming down pretty good. It's going to be a long drive." Gale observed as she looked out the window.

"I'll call for back up." Anna said as she grabbed the phone.

"Where are you going?" Gale asked as Daren headed to the door.

"To see what I have with me in the truck."

"OK Benton and Chris are on their way." Anna looked around.

"He went to his truck."

"OK I have my pistol and shot gun."

"What? You don't think?" Gale looked horrified.

"You never know mom."

A few minutes later Benton and Chris were both there.

"Let's go men." Daren said as he headed out the door, Anna followed.

"What. Where do you think you are going?" Benton stopped her.

"That's my boy, if you think I am staying here you are crazy."

The three of them looked at each other.

"OK you ride with me, You two follow in Chris's truck." Daren said.

"Then I'll wait here." Gale said looking scared.

"OK mom, love you." Daren kissed her on the head.

"Please be careful." She said looking like she might cry.

"We will." He said as they went out the door.

They headed down the road. They had decided to take both trucks in case one got stuck.

"Where did you say we are going again?" Anna asked trying to calm her nerves, as he drove faster than he should have been on the snowy roads.

"Just outside of Richfield."

"I see." Anna took out her phone and made a call.

Daren looked confused at her, but she just held up a finger.

"Hello, Aunt Ruth. So sorry to call so late, but we have a situation you may be able to help with."

"Sure, honey what is it?"

"Do you know a Wade…. I'm not sure of his last name."

"Baker." Daren chimed in.

"Wade Baker, he has his own business I believe. I never met him. Why?"

"Long story, but Trey is with him, and needs to be saved. We believe he is right outside of Richfield somewhere."

"I believe he has a small piece of property right outside of town. I think it only has a pole shed on it though."

"How do we get there?"

"There is a small convenience store just as your coming into town. I'll meet you there."

"Thank you, aunt Ruth."

"It's for my God Son. No thanks needed."

The snow seemed to be coming down harder and Anna grabbed the dash.

"Honey if we wreck and die, we can't save Trey."

"I know." He sighed and slowed down.

Chapter Sixty-Two

Trey slowly sat down on the bed. He felt like he might be sick. The thought of just beating the crap out of him occurred to him again, but what then. He was still stuck there with nowhere to go. What if that limo driver had a gun and came in. Was he still here? He wasn't sure. Wait, what if he had a gun in here somewhere? He was crazy. He didn't want to die this way.

"That's a good boy." Wade rubbed Trey's back pulling his tucked in shirt out of his pants.

Trey felt his skin crawl, and he just wanted to run, to fight do anything but this. He hung his head as he fought back tears.

"Don't cry, I promise I will take good care of you, my boy." Wade slipped his hand under his shirt and rubbed his bare back some more.

"Why are you doing this to me?" Trey said in a low voice.

Wade grabbed him by the chin and turned his face to him.

"I love you." With that he kissed Trey softly on the lips.

"I don't love you." Trey said as Wade finished the kiss.

"You will." Wade said as he pushed him back on the bed and straddled him. Holding his wrists above his head and looking into his eyes. "I told you I always get what I want."

Trey could see the craziness in his dark blue eyes, but there was also a soft side, hidden deep, it almost made Trey feel like maybe in some weird, crazy way he did love him. Maybe I could use this Trey thought. His mind raced to come up with a plan.

"I'm going to take good care of my boy." Wade said as he kissed Trey's neck and unbuttoned his shirt at the same time. He slowly started to move down his chest.

"Do you think this is a little fast?" Trey muttered.

"What?" Wade looked up at him as he tried to smile.

"Not that I'm not enjoying this um, sir." Trey smiled at him.

"Sir, I like that. You're a good boy." Wade smiled at him now, and moved up so they were face to face.

"I just think that we should take this slowly. I'm not a hundred percent um, ready I guess." He wasn't sure what else to say.

"I've been ready for you for some time." He leaned in and kissed him hard this time. Grabbing the back of his head and forcing his way into his mouth. With nowhere to go Trey went with it as much as he could force himself to.

"Good kisser." Wade said as he came up for air.

"Um, you to." Trey smiled.

"You to what?" He grabbed Trey by the jaw.

At first Trey was confused, "Um, Sir."

"That's my good boy." He slapped Trey's face. "Now don't be forgetting that, I would hate to punish you."

"No, sir." Trey didn't want to imagine what a punishment would be.

"Stand up." Wade said as he got off of him.

"What?" Trey looked confused.

Wade was on top of him again and grabbed him by the neck. "Does boy need punished?"

"No, sir. Sorry sir." Trey was thinking he may have started down a bad road.

"Now, stand up." Wade was up off of him again. Trey stood and looked at him.

"Turn around boy, show yourself off for me."

"Yes, sir." Trey said slowly and started to slowly turn.

"My boy is so cute." Wade grabbed his ass as he turned. Then he stopped him as he faced him, and just looking him in the eyes.

"Sir?"

"Why does my boy want to go slow?"

"I'm just not ready. I want to know you better first."

"I think you're just stalling. I'm going to have you boy." He grabbed his shirt and ripped it the rest of the way open, sending buttons flying.

"What the hell." Trey blurted out.

"That's not a good boy." Wade grabbed Trey's arm and turned him sideways and smacked his ass hard. Trey was in shock for a minute, not believing what just happened.

"Sorry, sir." Trey said fighting everything he had not to beat the crap out of him.

"That's better boy." He went to take his arm, but Trey walked away and went over to the window. He turned and looked at Wade.

"What is it boy?"

"If I wanted to be your boy, what do you want from me, Sir?" Trey thought he would try and keep him talking until he could come up with something to get himself out of this mess.

"I want you to live with me boy, to be there whenever I call you."

"But I have the farm, Sir."

"We would turn that into a housing development. I would take care of your every need."

"What would I do, Sir?"

"You would be at home. When I come home you will take care of me."

"Take care of you?"

"Come here, boy. I'll show you."

"Can't you just tell me?" He really didn't want to know what he was talking about.

"You didn't say sir, twice boy." Wade had his hand tightly on Trey's jaw before he knew what was happing. "Do I have to punish boy again?"

"No, sir. Sorry sir." Trey said through his teeth.

"Now, you need to be a good boy. I don't like punishing you." He said as he slapped Trey's face roughly.

"Yes, sir." Trey's mind was racing, he couldn't believe what was happening.

"I'll have my driver go to your place and pack your clothes for you."

"What...Sir?" Trey was more confused.

"You are mine now. You will not ask questions. You will do as you are told."

"Uh, no I'm not. Let me stop you right there." Trey put up his hand.

"Are you back talking boy?"

"Sir, I never agreed to any of this. I already said I have a boyfriend."

"That ended tonight with a phone call."

"What? Just who the hell do you think you are?" Trey glared at him now, his anger overflowing, he had had enough.

In seconds Wade had him on the floor his hand behind his back and Trey was in pain screaming.

Chapter Sixty-Three

Daren fought to see through the snow that seemed to never end.

"Look out!" Anna yelled as she pointed.

"I see!" Daren yelled as he took the truck off of the interstate and into a snow bank. Snow flew everywhere as they both bounced off the dash. They both sat motionless for a moment then there was a knock at the window.

"Hi officer." Daren said as he put the window down.

"Are you two OK" The officer who looked tired from long hours asked.

"Yes, we are fine."

"Bad night to be out. Big wreck two semis and six cars. You're going to be stuck here for a while I'm afraid." Chris and Benton were behind the officer now.

"OK Thank you officer." Anna said as Daren just stared at him.

The officer tipped his hat and walked away.

"What are we going to do?" Daren felt tears coming to his eyes.

"Not much we can do right now. Why don't you boys hop in here. Save your gas." Anna said as she rubbed Daren's back.

Minutes later they were all in the truck together.

"I could try and go off road." Daren said looking for the others to agree.

"The police would stop you." Chris sighed.

"I feel so helpless." Daren put his head on the steering wheel.

"Hello." Anna said into her phone, and they all looked at her.

"Anna darling where are you?" Ruth replied.

"Stuck. There is a major accident."

"Are you all alright?"

"Yes, but it's going to be a while before we get moving again."

"Not to worry. I will figure something out here."

"Don't do anything stupid and get yourself hurt."

"Now honey, would I?"

"Yes, please wait for us."

"OK dear."

"I'm going to go so I don't kill my phone."

"OK let me know when you are on the move again."

"We will, bye."

"What did she say?" Daren looked hopeful.

"She is going to save him."

"What? By herself?" Chris protested.

"No, I know her better than that. She has lots of friends. She will figure out something."

"But you told her to stay put." Daren was confused.

"Oh, please she never listens." Anna laughed.

Ruth sat in her truck at the gas station frustrated.

"That man has my God son. I have to save him." She got out of the truck and went into the store for a coffee. As she was adding sugar to her coffee three young men entered, and she smiled. One was over six foot tall and looked like a linebacker. He had dirty blond hair and brown eyes. The other two were shorter but still well built, with black hair and green eyes.

"Josh, how are you this evening?" She said to the tallest one.

"Fine miss Ruth. What are you doing out in this weather?"

"Looking for help."

"Why, what's wrong?"

"Do you happen to know a guy named Wade Baker?"

With that name the other two turned and looked at her.

"Yes, he isn't very well liked. Why do you ask?" Josh had a look of concern on his face.

"Well, it's kind of a long story, but my God son is with him and needs to be rescued."

"I see, he is a very unstable man." Josh sighed.

"And well versed in several kinds of martial arts." One of the other boys added.

"I'm afraid he may hurt my God son. If you don't go with me, I'll go by myself. I know where is property is."

The three boys looked at each other.

"Go pick up Dave." He pointed to the other two who just nodded. "Meet us there."

"Who is Dave?" Anna asked.

"He is also well versed in martial arts. We may need his help."

"Will he help us?"

"Yes, he hates Wade."

The two of them headed to Ruth's truck and the other two were gone already. A short time later they sat in the truck looking at a pole barn. There was smoke coming out of a small smoke stack at the back of the shed. A limo sat outside running.

"Well at least we know he is there." Josh smiled.

"I hope Trey is OK." Ruth looked worried.

"If he is related to you. I am sure he can take care of himself." Josh smiled at her, not sure if he even believed what he said.

A short time later the other three joined them.

The snow was blowing in Ruth's face, but she could still see the concentration in Dave's face as he walked over. He was medium build with black hair peeking out from under his hat. She was pretty sure he was Asian, but was hard to tell in this storm.

"Ruth this is Dave." Josh smiled.

"Nice to meet you, sorry it's for this reason." Dave nodded toward her.

"Thank you for coming."

"I don't like Wade very much. I never thought he would go this far though. Let's save your God son."

"The driver is in the limo. We will have to take care of him first." Jost pointed out.

They snuck down to the limo, and Josh knocked on the window.

"Hey dude, my truck is stuck, can you help me?" Josh said pointing toward the road.

The limo driver looked around, and rolled his eyes.

"I'm just up there." Josh pointed toward the tail lights. "I just slid off the road."

"Why are you out in this?" The limo driver looked annoyed.

"Had to run for my mother's…pills." Jost didn't know what else to say.

"OK." He got out of the limo and the others were on top of him.

"What the hell?" He yelled as they zip tied his hands behind him and put a gag in his mouth.

"Where is my God son?!" Ruth screamed at him.

They all looked as a phone on the front seat was going off. Josh grabbed in and it read my future husband.

"Hello." Josh answered it.

"No, we are going after him."

"Give it to me." Ruth reached for the phone.

"Help me put him in the back seat." Dave said to the rest of the guys.

"Hi, honey it's Ruth…. I know I said I would wait, but I got help… It's good we will see you when you get here."

"I'm guessing this is his coat." Josh held up a coat from the back seat.

"Get off of me!" Came a scream from the building behind them.

"That was him." Ruth turned.

"Don't go rushing in. He is quick and will hurt you." Dave grabbed her arm.

"Stop!" Trey yelled again.

Ruth turned and looked at Dave, and they started to move slowly toward the building.

Chapter Sixty-Four

"I said get off of me!" Trey scrambled away from him on his hands and knees.

"Where are you going?" Wade grabbed his pants and drug him back toward him.

"What is wrong with you?" Trey said as he kicked Wade in the crotch sending him stumbling backwards. Trey got to his feet tripped landing with his back against the wall.

"You will pay for that." Wade said as he pulled himself together.

The door beside Trey burst open.

"Leave him alone!" Ruth said as she was the first one through.

The surprise was enough that Wade didn't notice Dave at first.

"Aunt Ruth." Trey breathed a sigh of relief.

"Dave you should not have gotten involved." Wade turned his attention to him.

"Wade, what are you doing. You have always been odd, but this is over the top." Dave stood calmly looking at him.

"It's none of your business." Wade mirrored his calmness.

"It is my business; this is my God son." Ruth turned toward Wade. "You have picked the wrong God Mother to mess with."

"I love your God son, and in time he will learn to love me." Wade glared at her.

"I won't!" Trey yelled at him.

"What happen to you?" Dave moved slowly toward him.

"Come with us." Josh said to Trey and one of the other guys grabbed Ruth's arm. They move swiftly toward the door as Dave and Wade continued their conversation.

"We are going to go now. If your smart you will not follow."

"You're not taking my boy without a fight." Wade said as he darted toward the door. Ruth pushed everyone faster through the door trying to closed it as she left. Wade grabbed the door. Dave was on top of him.

"You need help!" Ruth said as she pushed the door into Wade as hard as she could causing him to stumble back. Dave grabbed him and had him pinned on the floor in seconds. Ruth pulled the door shut and followed the others outside.

"Here is your coat." Josh handed Trey his coat.

"How did you know?" Trey was almost in tears.

"Daren called; they tracked Wades phone." Ruth said as she hugged him.

They heard furniture crashing in the building.

"We need to go." Josh said.

"What about Dave?" Ruth protested.

"They are going to stay and help him." Josh pointed to the other two guys. "They both know karate as well."

"I hope those boys are OK." Ruth said as she made coffee.

"They will be fine; they had had run ins with him before."

Trey had been sitting with his head on the table.

"Are you OK. honey?" Ruth sat a coffee in front of him. He didn't answer or move at all.

"Is there anything broken, do you need to go to the hospital?" Josh asked.

"No." Trey said barely loud enough for anyone to hear.

"Honey, do you want to call Daren now?" Ruth asked. "He is very worried about you."

Trey didn't answer or move again. Just slowly pulled out his phone, and looked at it. Josh's phone went off and he took it into the living room.

"I kept praying somehow, I would be saved before he hurt me somehow. He was getting more and more." Trey stopped talking for a minute. "I just kept praying."

"Honey it's OK you are safe now." Ruth rubbed his back.

"Dave is safe. He is coming here." Josh said as he came back into the room.

"He was going to." Trey stopped and looked at his God mother.

"I know baby. Your safe now."

"We will call the cops in the morning and file a report, get charges…"

"I don't think I can go through that." Trey put his hand up.

"But honey." Ruth protested.

"I don't want to have to relive it."

Ruth's phone went off.

"Hi, honey. Yes, he is safe at my house. You want to talk to him?" Ruth looked at Trey who reached for the phone. Ruth motioned Josh to follow her to the living room to give Trey some privacy.

"You don't think he will try and find him, do you?" Ruth asked after they got into the living room.

"Not tonight, the limo won't go in this snow very well. Me and the boys are going to stay the night anyway."

"Thank you."

Chapter Sixty-Five

"Baby, are you OK?" Daren asked as he held the phone for everyone in the truck to hear.

"I am now. I'm sorry I ruined tonight." Trey started to say.

"You didn't ruin anything. I'm just glad your safe."

"Honey, we are trying to get there we are stuck in the snow."

"Mom?"

"Yes, honey we are all worried about you."

"Who is we?"

"Well uncle Chris and Benton are with us as well."

"Oh my God you guys be careful." Trey couldn't believe they all came to save him.

"Hold on there is an officer knocking on our window."

"Sir, we are going to have you follow this plow to the next exit where you have to get off the interstate."

"OK Sir." Daren smiled.

"I suggest that you find a hotel there and spend the night."

"We will officer. Thank you for your help." Daren said as he put his window back up.

"We will jump in our truck and follow you." Chris said as he and Benton got out of the truck.

"What's going on?" Trey's voice came across the phone.

"We are starting to move. I'll call you back in a while. Love you."

"Love you to." Trey said as he hung up.

"So, what's going on?" Ruth asked looking at him.

"They are starting to move. Following a plow now I think."

"I hope they are careful." Ruth shook her head not liking that they were on the move again.

Soon the boys were there and they all decided to camp out in the living room.

"The only thing he has is that limo. It isn't going anywhere in this weather." Josh reassured Ruth.

"I just can't believe how crazy this is."

Trey crawled on the couch and tossed and turned as he slept. Slowly one by one the others crawled on the floor with blankets till just Josh and Ruth were left sitting at the table.

"What do you think is going to happen?" Josh looked at Ruth who was looking off into space.

"I don't know." She sat her coffee down and looked at Josh. "I don't like the possibilities though. I'm worried he isn't going to stop."

"That family all has mental issues."

"I have been praying all night for a way to keep Trey safe."

"What was that noise?" Josh said as they both raced to the window.

"Fire truck and an ambulance. That's not good."

"Well Daren said when he called back, that they stopped for the night at the red roof inn." Josh rubbed Ruth's back.

"I know." She looked at him and nervously smiled.

"We are safe here. I promise." Josh walked her to the stairs. "Why don't you go to bed. In the light of day all will seem better."

Trey felt like he had just laid down and there was a knock at the door. He sat straight up. Looking around the guys were gone. He walked into the kitchen and saw no one, and the knock came again.

"Don't answer that." Ruth's voice came from behind him.

"Who is it?" Trey asked afraid of the answer.

"Where are the boys?" Ruth looked around confused.

"I'm not sure. They weren't here when I woke up."

The knocking came on the door again. "I know you have my husband." Came Wade's voice. Trey froze in fear. Where had the guys gone? Was the only thing that was running through his mind.

"Please Aunt Ruth go upstairs. I don't want you getting hurt."
"I'll do no such thing."
"I'll just go with him. I won't let him hurt you."
"He will hurt you."
The knocking came again, harder this time.
"Your boys already tried to stop me. No one will stop me."
"I have no choice. I'm not going to let him hurt anyone else."
"Trey no!"

Trey opened the door and Wade stood there covered in dirt, snow and blood. He grabbed Trey by the throat and pulled him in.

"This is all your fault. You will be punished boy."
"I'm sorry!" Trey yelled.
"Trey Honey." Ruth grabbed him.

Trey jumped and opened his eyes. The sun was coming through the windows. The snow had stopped. He was covered in sweat.

"Honey you were having a dream. I made breakfast, come get something to eat."

Trey nodded and in a few minutes was sitting at the table with the guys. He just played with his food pushing it around on his plate.

"I really think you need to call the cops honey. You're not going to feel safe until you do." Ruth finally said breaking the silence.

"I know." Trey sighed.

There was a knock at the door and Trey almost jumped right out of his seat.

"It's ok. It's just Daren and the rest of them." Ruth smiled as she got up.

Trey ran to the door and opened it. Daren grabbed him and gave him a big hug and just held on tightly.

Chapter Sixty-Six

"Listen honey, we will call the cops and this will all be over." Anna rubbed his back.

"Yes, officer that is who I want to make a complaint about." Ruth said looking confused. "OK fine we will be here waiting."

"What did he say?" Josh asked before anyone else could.

"He said very interesting and asked if he could come talk to us." Ruth said as she laid her phone down.

"You don't think he made a complaint about us first." Trey looked nervous.

"That would leave him with a lot of explaining to do." Anna shook her head.

"Yeah, like how did you get down here in the first place." Daren spoke up.

"Let's just wait for the officer, and not jump to any conclusions." Ruth said as she poured herself a cup of coffee.

They didn't have to wait long, the officer knocked on the door and was led into the kitchen.

"Would you like a coffee?" Ruth offered.

"No thank you ma'am. You said that Mr. Baker had kidnapped someone?"

"Yes, that would be my son. Trey." Anna smiled.

"And where is he?"

"I'm right here."

"How did this kidnapping happen?"

Trey explained what happened.

"That would be hard to make a case of."

"But he lied to him.." Anna started to protest.

"He did, but he also said he was free to go. Even if he made it almost impossible for him to do so."

Everyone kind of hung there head a little.

"It really doesn't make much difference now." The officer looked around the room at the confused looks on everyone's face.

"What do you mean by that?" Ruth finally asked.

"After you boys left Mr. Baker last night, he got his limo unstuck. He was most likely looking for you. He was angry I guess and was driving at a high rate of speed, going off the road and down an embankment during the night."

Ruth and Josh looked at each other. The officer seeing them nodded.

"Yes, they were the sirens you heard. It was just up the road where he wrecked."

"So where is he now?" Trey looked scared.

"Him nor the driver made it. We were trying to figure out why the driver was bound with zip ties, but you cleared that up."

"You mean he died?" Trey looked relieved.

"Yes, I'm afraid so."

It was a mixed reaction of relief and disbelief flying around the room.

"If I have any further question whom should I contact?"

"Just call me officer." Ruth took a pen and wrote her number down.

"Thank you all. I'm sorry for what happen to you. I hope you can get some closure." The officer looked at Trey.

"Yes, thank you." Trey smiled at him.

The officer nodded to everyone and Ruth walked him to the door.

Nobody said anything for a while. They all had thoughts running through their minds.

"Um, I hope you don't mind but me and the boys are going to be going." Josh finally said.

"Oh, yes. Thank you for all your help." Ruth hugged each of them.

"Yes, thanks for the rescue." Trey shook each of their hands, fighting off the urge to bear hug each of them. Anna gave each of them a hug as well and the boys were gone.

"Aunt Ruth I'm sorry for dragging you into all of this." Trey said after a few minutes of silence.

"Honey, I love you. I will always be there for you. Besides it's good the get this old ticker going sometimes. Makes me feel alive." Ruth walked over and hugged Trey.

"I am really tired, do you thing we can head home?" Trey looked at Daren and Anna.

"Yes, I agree." Anna smiled at Ruth. "Thank you again."

"Honey we are family. I will always be there for you. Now get going, I have things to get done today as well." Ruth smiled and hugged each of them as they left.

Chapter Sixty-Seven

Spring was in the air. The cold days of winter were fading into memory as well as the dark dreams of Wade. The officer had contacted Ruth and said the case had been closed. Trey had started seeing a councilor about the dreams he was having, and it seemed to be helping. The land next to them that Wade owned was now up for sale, and that seemed to really help Trey move on.

"You know we could have some fun in here." Daren came up behind Trey who was cleaning the floor of the barn.

"Don't push me into that hay again." Trey pretended to try and stop him.

They were both soon in the hay holding each other and kissing.

"I love you so much." Daren looked deep into his eyes, holding Trey's face so he couldn't look away. This always sent waves of electricity through Trey and he smiled without realizing it.

Daren turned and jumped-up pulling Trey to his feet.

"What are you doing?" Trey was confused.

"Trey, would you make me the happiest man alive." Daren started and he pulled out a small box and got on one knee. "I don't want anyone else in my life but you. I want us to grow old together running this farm. Will you be my husband?" Daren opened the box and presented him a gold ring that looked like binder twine.

"Oh, my god where did you get this?" Trey took it out of the box, and put it on.

"Answer him!" came several voices from outside the barn.

"Yes!" Trey laughed and hugged Daren as all the family came running in.

"We have a wedding to plan!" Anna shouted then kissed both guys.

They moved outside the barn where everything was set up for a picnic to celebrate.

They partied for hours and blasted music. As the evening died down Anna came over to Trey.

"Baby, I couldn't be happier for you." She hugged him.

"Thank you, mom." Trey hugged her back. "There is a but in there though."

"Aunt Ruth wanted to be here, but she isn't feeling well."

"I know she is always with me." Trey smiled at her.

"Honey, she had a stroke this morning. She is in the hospital."

Trey just looked at her and could see in her eyes it wasn't good.

"I want to go see her."

"I know. I'm sorry."

"I'm going first thing in the morning."

"I'll go with you. Honey, I have the address."

"I'll take care of the farm baby."

Trey turned to see Daren standing there.

"Go with your mom baby. I know how important she is to you."

Trey looked at his mom.

"We will leave first thing in the morning."

Sleep didn't come fast for Trey and when he finally fell asleep noises woke him. He opened his eyes and looked around. He was in the barn, but the old baler was there. He looked around confused. The old baler had been sold how did it get back here. Then realized he didn't even know how he got to the barn. He was in bed.

"Oh, honey you really don't know how?"

Trey turned to see Aunt Ruth walking from the back of the barn.

"I don't like this." Trey's eyes saddened.

"Look at this old rusty baler. Should have retired it years ago, but your father." Ruth looked away from the baler to Trey.

"You're not old and rusty." Trey said knowing where she was going.

"Honey, my time is short. The good lord is calling me home."

"But..."

"No, buts. No one has control over when it's their time. I learned that a while back." She picked up the cross that hung around her neck with her husband's ashes in it. "I can't wait to see him again."

"I'm going to miss you. Who is going to look out for me now?" Trey tried to smile.

"You don't need me anymore. Daren loves you. Besides we will meet again."

"I hope so."

"Keep right with God. Pray every day."

"I know."

"We will meet again." She kissed him on the forehead and walked toward the back of the barn and was gone.

"She's right you know."

Trey turned to see his dad standing there.

"Yeah, I will see you all again."

"No, this mess should have been retired years ago." He threw the wrench he was holding and he was gone.

Trey opened his eyes, happy to have seen his dad again, but saddened that Aunt Ruth's time was short.

He went downstairs and his mom was sipping coffee. He could see she had been crying. He just went over and hugged her.

Chapter Sixty-Eight

Aunt Ruth's services came and went and the farm was going as spring started to turn to summer, and they stayed busy enough they had no time to think about anything else.

"You know we need to talk about your wedding." Anna said as they both came in for lunch one day.

"I know mom. We really just want something small." Trey smiled at her as he sat down.

"Yeah, just close family, maybe a few friends." Daren added.

"Yes, I know that is what you guys said, but Gale and I have ideas."

"They should not be allowed to play together." Trey smiled at Daren.

"Just let us plan everything. All you have to do is show up."

"But keep is small." Daren reminded her.

"Small yes." Anna smiled.

"Oh, this is not going to go the way we want it." Trey shook his head as he ate his burger.

"So, is there anyone you absolutely want there?"

"I don't think it matters much. You're going to invite whoever you want anyway." Trey said as he swallowed his burger. Daren laughed and continued to eat his burger.

"You think you're so funny, well we will invite who ever we want then." Anna picked up her notebook and went outside.

"Oh, shit she got into the car with my mom." Daren said as he looked out the window.

"I said they shouldn't be allowed to play together." Trey laughed.

The day of the wedding came and Trey and Daren looked at what seemed like hundreds of chairs that had been set up in the yard. Daren had stayed with his mom the night before, at her request, because it was bad luck for him to see Trey the day of. So, Daren was now in the barn, where they had made a make shit room for him to get ready.

Trey was standing in the kitchen looking out over the yard at the tents that had been set up the day before.

"Mom this is too much." Trey shook his head. "What happen to small?"

"Well part of that is for the service and part is for the reception. So, in reality it's not all that big." Anna smiled at him.

"I can't believe you did all of this."

"Your brothers were a big help."

"Where are they anyway?"

"They all have parts to play and are busy making sure everything is right."

"They are going to make me pay for this."

"Nonsense. Now stand up straight so I can see if your tie is right."

Trey took a deep breath and let her fuss at him for the hundredth time.

"Are you ready?" Clayton said as he stuck his head in the door.

"Yes, let's do this." Trey smiled.

Clayton walked Trey out, while Eddie walked Daren. Stan had gone on line and got ordained, and he performed the ceremony. There was enough food for the whole state at the reception. The pictures took to long for Trey, who hated his picture taken. But soon they were mingling with the guest, and eating. The first dance happened and the other wedding traditions. The night was winding down.

"Congrats."

Trey turned to see Peter and Ashley standing there.

"Peter. I can't..."

"I know." Peter smiled at him.

"Hi Ashley it is so good to see you." Trey knelt down to her. She smiled and looked at her daddy, then ran.

"I didn't know you were here."

Peter looked a little confused.

"Oh, mom took care of everything. I didn't know who she invited."

"I wanted to talk to you earlier, but didn't know if you wanted to talk to me."

"Of course I would talk to you." Trey looked around.

"Yeah, Valery isn't here. We broke up after the new year."

"Oh, sorry to hear that."

"Well, you were right. She wanted her name on the business, and when I told her it was in my mom's name and I had nothing." Peter just half smiled at him.

"I know. It's all good. I'm very happy to see you." He hugged Peter.

"Yeah, well I have been through two other girlfriends since."

"The right one will come along soon enough."

"Funny thing. When I got your invite, my mother said to me. That could have been you."

Trey looked confused and waited for more.

"I guess she has known for a long time, but was waiting for me to come out."

"I see."

"She got tired of waiting and told me to deal with who I am and make myself happy. That I needed to set that example for Ashely."

"So, what are you going to do?"

"Start a new Journey it seems."

"And what a journey you will have. Come let's have some fun. I have friends to introduce you to."

Other books by Donald L. Marino

The Journey Series
    Carl's Journey (Book one)
    Benton's Journey (Book two)
    Trey's Journey (Book Three)

The Shadow Series
    Return of the Shadows The Chosen Book one
    Return of the Shadows Under Attack Book Two
    Return of the Shadows The Final Stand Book Three
    Return of the Shadows Breaking the Spell Book Four

Short Stories
    I was prompted to write these stories.

Children's book.
    Tinsel's First Snow Fall

About the Author

Donald L Murray Jr. was born in central Pennsylvania. As a senior in high school, Donald wrote his first book, a Hardy boy's style book, that got him an A in English class. Donald spent four years in the Army, where he lived in Germany, as well as being involved in the first gulf war. Since coming home, he moved to northeast Pennsylvania where Donald was involved with community theater for over twelve years as well as taking an improve class in New York City. Donald married his husband, Anthony, and took his last name, Marino. Besides sitting at home writing Donald also loves to travel. Donald's favorite author is Terry Brooks.

www.ingramcontent.com/pod-product-compliance
Lightning Source LLC
LaVergne TN
LVHW021803060526
838201LV00058B/3213